N • CRIME SEEN • CR

**For more information on Michaelbrent's
books, including specials and sales; and for
info about
signings, appearances, and media,**

**check out his webpage,
"Like" his Facebook fanpage
or
Follow him on Twitter.**

"Collings is so proficient at what he does, he crooks his finger to get you inside his world and before you know it, you are along for the ride. You don't even see it coming; he is that good." – *Only Five Star Book Reviews*

"Collings' most polished and horrific tale to date." – horrornews.net

"Move over Stephen King... Clive Barker.... Michaelbrent Collings is taking over as the new king of the horror book genre." – *Media Mikes*

"*STRANGERS* is another white-knuckled journey that demands to be read in one sitting." – *The Horror Fiction Review*

"Michaelbrent spins a tale that keeps you enthralled from page to page.... Overall I give this novel an A." – *The Horror Drive-In*

DARKBOUND

"Really good, highly recommended, make sure you have time to read a lot at one sitting since you may have a hard time putting it down." – *The Horror Fiction Review*

"In *Darkbound* you will find the intensity of *Misery* and a journey reminiscent of the train ride in *The Talisman*.... A proficient and pedagogical author, Collings' works should be studied to see what makes his writing resonate with such vividness of detail.... You will not be disappointed in this dark tale." – *Hellnotes*

"A spell-binding conclusion comes from out of nowhere that is hauntingly reminiscent of M. Night Shyamalan or Alfred Hitchcock. A certifiable bone chiller...." – horrornews.net

"*Darkbound* travels along at a screaming pace with action the whole way through, and twists to keep you guessing throughout.... With an ending that I didn't see coming from a mile away, and easily one of the best I've had the enjoyment of reading in a long time...." – *Horror Drive-In*

THE HAUNTED

"*The Haunted* is a terrific read with some great scares and a shock of an ending!" – Rick Hautala, international bestselling author; Bram Stoker Award® for Lifetime Achievement winner

"[G]ritty, compelling and will leave you on the edge of your seat.... *The Haunted* is a tremendous read for fans of ghoulishly good terror." – horrornews.net

"*The Haunted* is just about perfect.... This is a haunted house story that will scare even the most jaded horror hounds. I loved it!" – Joe McKinney, Bram Stoker Award®-winning author of *Flesh Eaters* and *The Savage Dead*

APPARITION

"*Apparition* is not just a 'recommended' novel, it is easily one of the most entertaining and satisfying horror novels this reviewer has read within the past few years. I cannot imagine that any prospective reader looking for a new read in the horror genre won't be similarly blown away by the novel." – *Hellnotes*

"[*Apparition* is] a gripping, pulse hammering journey that refuses to relent until the very final act. The conclusion that unfolds may cause you to sleep with the lights on for a spell.... Yet be forewarned perhaps it is best reserved for day time reading." – horrornews.net

"*Apparition* is a hard core supernatural horror novel that is going to scare the hell out of you.... This book has everything that you would want in a horror novel.... it is a roller coaster ride right up to a shocking ending." – horroraddicts.net

"[*Apparition* is] Riveting. Captivating. Mesmerizing.... [A]n effective, emotional, nerve-twisting read, another amazingly well-written one from a top-notch writer." – *The Horror Fiction Review*

THE LOON

"It's always so nice to find one where hardcore asylum-crazy is done RIGHT.... *THE LOON* is, hands down, an excellent book." – *The Horror Fiction Review*

"Highly recommended for horror and thriller lovers. It's fast-moving, as it has to be, and bloody and violent, but not disgustingly gory.... Collings knows how to write thrillers, and I'm looking forward to reading more from him." – *Hellnotes*

MR. GRAY (AKA THE MERIDIANS)

"... an outstanding read.... This story is layered with mystery, questions from every corner and no answers fully coming forth until the final conclusion.... What a ride.... This is one you will not be able to put down and one you will remember for a long time to come. Very highly recommended." – *Midwest Book Review*

RUN

"[A] tense and intense scary sci-fi chiller/thriller.... RUN is a winner, as fast-paced as it should be, cinematic and gripping, lots of fun but with moments of poignancy and disturbing paranoia." – *The Horror Fiction Review*

HOOKED: A TRUE FAERIE TALE

"*Hooked* is a story with depth.... Emotional, sad, horrific, and thought provoking, this one was difficult to put down and now, one of my favourite tales." – *Only Five Star Book Reviews*

RISING FEARS

DEDICATION

To...

Tom, Russ, and Jess, who let a complete stranger on their show, and then started reading his books,

my Grampas, who were great examples of Real Men,

and to Laura, FTAAE.

Contents

CRIME

Evan White looked at his hands again, as though this time he might see something different. As though this time they might hold answers; might tell him where his life had gone and how everything had turned to crap so very quickly.

For the briefest instant it seemed like he was on the edge of an epiphany. An understanding that would shift not merely his perception but his existence.

"I'm the one you've been looking for."

The voice sounded in Evan's head, the memory bouncing around like a bullet in his skull, ripping apart bits of his mind. Peeling away his brain a layer at a time, drilling deep, revealing... what?

The call had come on his cell phone. Just one more call, like so many that had come in the wake of... in the wake of what had happened.

Tragedy brings out the worst in humanity. It brings out the leeches and the sycophants and the crazies. At first Evan thought that the call came from another one of the latter: just one more nut-job who had seen the case in the paper and wanted five seconds of vicarious fame. In a world where heiresses could sex their way to stardom and ninety percent of prime time news seemed to be devoted to what some anorexic starlet was wearing, Evan shouldn't have been surprised. Shouldn't have been disappointed.

But he was. He felt his spirit die a bit with every call.

"Do you have a name?" he said.

The phone had sat silent in his hand for a moment. That was the first time he thought he might be talking to someone out of the ordinary. Not that he believed for a second it was *the* someone. No. But maybe not a nutter, either. Nutters talked too much, answered too quickly. A simple "Do you have a name?" would have been an invitation for a torrent of crazy, a deluge of insanity.

Not silence.

Finally, the man on the other end of the phone said, "That's not important. What's important is the look on your wife's face when she died."

Evan went cold when he heard those words. Maybe the man on the phone was a kook. But Evan had to know.

He had to.

"Is this a joke to you?" he said.

The man laughed. And the laugh was the thing that cinched it, the thing that guaranteed that Evan would go where the man wanted him to go, on the off chance that he actually knew something.

Because whether this man was involved in the murder of Evan's wife or not, the laugh was the scraping, scratching howl of a madman. The shriek of a devil who hadn't quite figured out the best way to destroy his fill of happiness, to quench his fill of joy.

Evan didn't know what the man wanted, exactly. But the laugh told him that it involved pain. Misery.

Death.

The conversation played over and over in Evan's mind. It kept on turning and returning, spinning around until he had checked it from all angles, listening to it until he could hear no more.

Again he felt like he was on the edge of something, some realization that would... *matter.* That would even, perhaps, take away the image of his wife's face as it had been when he saw her last.

Then he realized it wasn't epiphany he perched on the edge of. No, just a barstool. Backless, the kind that would let you spin around on a whim. In better places that might be because you were hoping to find a romantic attachment, maybe just people-watch. Here, though, you could probably spin around forever and never find anything good to look at. Torn faux leather gouged at Evan's thighs and buttocks, biting through the cheap fabric of his suit pants, and a backless stool in this kind of place just meant you had a good chance of cracking your head open after the night's bender stole your backbone.

Evan looked at his drink again. Wondered if he should drink the rest. Probably not. He wasn't even sure what it was. This wasn't the kind of place you came to drink high-quality booze, it was the kind of place you came to drink angry and get angrier. The kind of place you came to get drunk, but what you ended up doing more often than not was getting in a fight.

It was small, poorly lit even by the low standards for this kind of place. A few tables – one or two even had chairs – and the bar. The bar itself was sticky, made of a wood that had been burnt and stained by countless old cigarette butts and spilled drinks and blood until it was a dark, grainless brown that might be oak or cherry or walnut or Formica laminate for all Evan could tell.

Bleed on a thing long enough, it stops being what it

was, and turns to just a faded brown bar in a bad part of town.

At the other end of the bar, a girl with short-cut hair that had been dyed in every color of the rainbow was holding the hand of a drunk. Evan thought at first she was a hooker, but something about her changed his mind. He couldn't see her face, but something about the way she held herself didn't say she was turning tricks.

"I'll read your palm one time," said Rainbow Hair. "*One* time."

The drunk snorted. He was a big guy, dressed in flannels and jeans that had seen lots of wear. Maybe a dock worker. "Can you really do this?" he said, every other word nearly a mumble.

"I've always seen the truth," said the girl in a tone that was too bright to belong in this bar.

The drunk laughed. "Tell me a lie. Lies are better."

You got that right, thought Evan. Then he turned away from the pair. They weren't what he was here for. They weren't who he was looking for.

"No worries," laughed the girl. "Whenever people see the truth, they always forget."

Evan's cell rang. The ring tone was one Val had picked. He hadn't changed it yet.

"White," he said into the phone, the typical answer he gave. He never needed more.

The voice that answered wasn't that of a lunatic in human shape. Evan didn't know if he was happy or sad about that. He felt confused, felt like he hadn't been able to get his head on straight since….

Since Val. Don't lie. Not to yourself.

Regardless, the voice that came from his cell was a comfortable one, though with a hard edge hiding just behind it. Evan always thought of those old pictures of Japanese samurai when he heard this voice: men who were honorable, who were good. Who moved slowly and deliberately... until it was time to attack. Then, God help anyone who got in their way.

"Anything?" Max Geist was as to-the-point on the phone as Evan was. Part of why they got along, he supposed: neither of them felt a need to pad their lives or conversation with things that weren't necessary.

Evan sensed motion at the bar's entrance. He wasn't sure how – perhaps he glimpsed it in the mirror behind the bar, a reflection torn apart by innumerable bottles in colorful glass. Maybe it was a trace sound he registered subconsciously.

Whatever it was, Evan spun on his seat. His free hand fell to his belt, brushing past the badge clipped there and circling the grip of the handgun holstered directly behind it.

His hand relaxed almost as fast as it had clenched. The movement wasn't someone entering, just someone leaving. The door to the bar had been propped open – apparently to better allow drunks and flies to find their way inside – and now Rainbow Hair was making her way out.

Evan wondered what she looked like.

He wondered why he cared.

He remembered Val's face.

He turned away from that thought, turned his attention back to Geist's question. "Nothing," he said. "Haven't seen anything."

He spun back to the bar. Sipped at his drink.

"Well, it was a long shot," said Geist. He sighed. "Don't stay up too late." And then he hung up. He didn't say goodbye.

Music had been playing on a juke box behind Evan. The song stopped at almost the same moment Geist hung up. Evan dragged his gaze away from the half-filled drink he had been nursing for what seemed an eternity.

Quarters clinked. He heard that hollow click-clack of jukebox keys being pushed.

And the same damn song started again. It was "You Spin Me Round" by Dead or Alive. Evan had nothing against the song – it was as good as anything from the late eighties could be – but he had heard it enough for one night.

"How many times you gonna listen to that?" he said.

The woman at the jukebox didn't even look at him.

"How many times you gonna keep listening to cranks?" she said. Her tones were clipped, almost harsh. Angela Listings, she of the Dead or Alive obsession, was Evan's partner. She was currently wearing no-nonsense jeans, a t-shirt, and a jacket bulky enough to hide her service revolver. But no amount of cumbersome, off-the-rack, shapeless clothing could hide her beauty or her attitude.

She was the kind of woman that men pursued... for about a minute and half. But most men didn't like that she could beat them in a fight of wits or of straight-out fists.

And she was the kind of girl you would take home to mother only if dear old Ma had a strong constitution and found perverse joy in meeting hard-ass bitches.

She turned to him now. Oval face, with a deep tan that

couldn't quite hide the small spatter of freckles across her nose. Eyes that Evan knew could be wide and inviting when Listings wanted them that way. Now they were at half-mast, hooded like those of a bored viper seriously considering a random strike just because-screw-it-that's-why. She was waiting for him to answer.

How many times *would* he answer these calls? How many times would he trudge down dead ends, follow the same paths that ultimately led nowhere?

He shook his head, shrugged his shoulders. "As many times as I have to."

Listings pursed her lips as though considering whether that answer was acceptable. Evan wondered what she'd do if she decided it wasn't. Probably just sucker punch him or bite his nose off or something.

Evidently he'd passed the test, though. She sat next to him. He raised his drink in mock salute and brought the glass to his lips.

She intercepted it. Grabbed the glass away from him in a smooth motion that spilled not a drop of the murky liquid within, and shook her finger at him.

"If we're here looking for a killer, then this is official business and you shouldn't be drinking," she said. Then she tossed back the drink.

"Thanks for the reminder," said Evan dryly. It figured that Listings would be able to throw back alcohol like a Russian sailor, too. She probably wrote her name in the snow, including dotting both "I"s.

"Lighten up," said Listings. "We've been here for over an hour. I don't think –"

"Hey!"

Listings and Evan both turned to find the drunk standing before them. Up close he was larger than he had seemed when seated at the other end of the bar. He was well over six feet tall, and Evan guessed he was upwards of two hundred fifty pounds.

He revised his earlier guess – the guy wasn't a dock worker, he was the *dock*.

The big man was weaving, blurry eyes fading in and out of focus as he loomed over Listings. But his finger, which was roughly the size of a horse's leg, was completely stable and in control as he jabbed it in her direction. "I know you," he said. He paused, apparently gathering his thoughts.

Evan took the moment to glance at Listings. She appeared completely at ease, leaning back on the bar, arms loose on the wood/Formica/whatever-it-was. A smile played about the edges of her lips, which worried Evan. It was rarely a good thing when Listings smiled.

"You're the bitch that keeps turning on that song," said the drunk. "I heard it, like…." He weaved again. Evan started to stand, hoping he could keep everyone from losing their cool.

The drunk shook himself. "… like, a billion times. *Bitch.*"

Listings slid off her stool. Evan would have stopped it if he could have, but it happened too quickly. His partner getting to her feet was akin to a country warning off its enemies by priming all its nukes and putting them on a countdown.

"Don't," said Evan.

Listings flashed him a smile. She was gorgeous, and everything that had happened with Val – not just her death, but the things she had done to him before she died – just made him more aware of that.

But under the beauty… danger.

"I got this," she said. Then turned to the drunk. "Don't like the song?" she said.

The drunk drew himself up even taller. Trying to stare down the woman who probably only weighed about half what he did. "Not after the first million times."

Listings moved uncomfortably close to the bear-man. In his face, in his space. "I thought it was a billion." Even drunk, Evan figured the guy had to hear the implicit, "Are you too dumb to even *count*?" in her tone.

The drunk blinked. For a moment he looked like he was going to back down. Evan really hoped that would happen. That would mean everyone left without broken bones or torn tendons or unnecessary trips to the hospital.

Then he blinked again. His eyes both focused on Listings at the same time – a small miracle considering the amount of booze the guy had probably pounded – and he sneered. "Whatever. Hey, I just figured why you like this song. You maybe want me to spin *you* around?"

He grabbed his crotch.

Evan sighed. He wanted to hide his face in his hands. He didn't, though. Partly because he felt a duty to keep an eye on his partner, no matter how much she didn't need it. Partly because what was coming was going to have all the horrific fascination of a train wreck. He just couldn't look away.

Listings laughed. It was an almost painful-sounding laugh, a rip-rattle laugh that made it clear she wasn't laughing *with* the drunk, she was laughing *at* him. "Classy," she said.

"I assume we're doing pantomimes because you're aware the smartest thing that ever came out of your mouth was a penis."

The big man's hand clenched on his own groin, as though shock had caused him to clutch desperately for some tangible reassurance of his own manhood. "Wha...?"

Before he could even process the first insult, let alone come up with a rejoinder, Listings had waded back in. She snapped her fingers. "Hey, I know you! I told your boyfriend his shoes were ugly and he tried to hit me with his purse. That was you, right?"

The drunk's hand remained clenched on the front of his pants. But his leer, which had frozen into a rictus of confusion, transformed to a snarl.

"Listings," said Evan. He didn't know what else he was going to say, what else he *could* say, but he felt like he should say something.

He suspected if he saw a tidal wave rushing down the center of Los Angeles, he'd probably feel the same urge to speak. And that it would probably have the same lack of effect.

"Don't worry, I'm not going to hit him," said Listings. For a moment Evan dared to hope that they might get out of here without things turning violent. Then her smile widened – bad to worse – and she turned back to the drunk and said, "That would be animal cruelty."

The drunk's snarl rippled over his entire body. His muscles clenched and he seemed to grow three inches in every direction.

Evan moved. Too slow. By the time he was up, by the time he had moved into position, it had already happened.

The drunk growled, sounding like a wounded animal that had turned deadly in the depths of its pain. He flung himself forward, moving faster than Evan expected. Not just big, not just strong, but *agile*.

He swung a fist the size of a radiator at Listings.

Evan's breath caught in his throat.

Don't kill him, Listings.

Listings moved like a drop of water skittering across a hot stove top. Evan could barely see her, she was so fast. One moment she was right in the path of the fist, the next... gone.

The drunk seemed as shocked as Evan at Listings' apparent magic act. She hadn't moved until the last second, the very final moment before he pummeled her out of existence. Now the momentum behind his punch combined with his inebriation to drive him stumbling forward.

The drunk slipped. Slammed face-first into the bar.

Crunch.

Evan winced as he heard the unmistakable sound of bones breaking. Hopefully just a nose.

The drunk slid to the floor between the stools that Evan and Listings had been sitting on a moment ago. His hand covered his face, and his eyes seemed to be spinning independently. He moaned, then slipped a bit lower.

"Dammit, Listings," said Evan.

"What?" A few locks of Listings' long brown hair had managed to pull loose from the rest of her mane. She pushed them back into place impatiently. "I didn't touch him. He slipped."

She bent over the drunk. Evan considered pointing out the fact that she had definitely arranged the circumstances so slipping would be a bit more *likely*, but decided it wouldn't do anything helpful and shut his mouth.

After five years with Listings, Evan had decided that a good partnership, like a good marriage, was often a matter of just shutting up and letting your significant other do whatever the hell she was going to do. He'd be there if anyone needed help. If not, he'd be there, too. Either way, getting in front of Listings was not a healthy idea.

"Come on, Betty Ford," said Listings. "Up you go."

The drunk continued his struggle to get both eyes pointed in one direction as he said, "Who you callin' Betty?"

He swiped at Listings with one blood-spattered hand. She dodged easily, but her face darkened and her smile returned. "You just don't learn, do you?"

"Listings, don't –"

Listings wasn't listening at all now. That the drunk had come on to her and accosted her was one thing. That he had tried to hit her after she had beaten him would be seen as unforgiveable.

Evan started trying to figure out which was the closest hospital with an emergency room.

Listings raised her fist. It was a small fist, but painfully angular, and several of the knuckles had rows of scars that attested to the fights she'd been in over the years. Evan didn't move to stop his partner now... not because he didn't have time, but because he genuinely didn't want to find out what a coma felt like.

Listings' hand dropped. Fast as a hornet, so fast Evan could almost hear the air split around it.

But it didn't connect.

Evan felt like the world, spinning along in its

predictable if generally horrible way, had suddenly reversed course. He had seen Listings in a lot of fights. He had *never* seen her fail to connect with something she tried to hit.

It wasn't that she missed, per se. It wasn't as though the drunk managed to slide away from her attack, to dodge her punch as she had dodged his only a moment ago.

No, something – some*one* – had stopped her. A hand had wrapped around her forearm, stalling her forward momentum, cutting off the attack before it could begin.

Listings looked over her shoulder at the stranger, her anger at the drunk transmuting into rage that someone would touch her.

"Let go of me," she said.

The man who had stopped her was normal-looking. A bit boring, even. Evan had never seen him before, and even if he had he doubted he would have recognized him. Brown eyes. Brown hair, thinning a bit at the temples and receding a bit along the forehead. And that was the sum total of the man's physical attributes. Brown on brown, boring on boring. Nothing to hold to mentally, nothing to remember.

He wore a black coat, and it *was* memorable. It was long and voluminous, seeming to flow like a living thing around the man's body, pulling light into it and giving nothing in return.

"Let go of me," said Listings again.

The man smiled. Boring smile. And Evan saw his eyes change. Not in size or shape, but where they had been empty before, now they were full of something terrifying. Madness.

"No," said the man.

"I said, let *go!*"

Evan was moving, but again he was too slow. The

instant he heard the man speak, heard him say, "No," he knew that this was the man he had spoken to on the phone. This was the man he had been looking for tonight.

But Listings was faster again. Faster, and too fast, and not fast enough.

She swung at the man, a quick cross with her free hand.

And for the second time tonight, she missed.

The man ducked. Spun her around.

Bright light glinted. Evan had his gun out, but the brightness froze him. It wasn't the brightness of a light being shone, but of something reflective. Something sharp.

The man had a knife at Listings' throat. And it was so sharp it grabbed the dim light of the bar and slashed it into a million glinting pieces.

"Don't move!" Evan shouted.

The man grinned. "Or what?" he said. He pressed on the knife. Not too hard, but even the light pressure made blood well around the blade and drip down Listings' neck. "You'll kill me?" He giggled. "How do you kill a man who's already dead?"

Evan didn't have time to digest the weirdness of that. Listings' eyes rolled as though she was mostly irritated with the whole situation. "Shoot him, White."

"Shut up, Listings," said Evan. To the man he said, "You're the one who called me?"

The man smiled. A boring smile, a banal smile. The mad, mundane smile of any of a million people who go about their lives quietly each day hoping no one will notice how close they are to breaking. "Don't ask questions you already know the answer to," he said.

Evan wondered if anyone had called 9-1-1. In this part of town, in a bar like this, he figured the chances were about even. Not good odds. "What do you want?" he said, as much to stall as anything.

Tears welled up in the other man's eyes. His lower lip quivered, and Evan thought he might have killed his partner with his question.

"For it to end," said the man.

The jukebox clicked. Listings had chosen "You Spin Me Round" too many times to count, and now the song was ending. Evan was gripped by the sudden belief that if the song she had chosen ended before he got her free, she would die.

The song was over.

Another began. And whether it was because Listings had pre-programmed it, or because of some cosmic joke, the same song started again.

Evan had completely forgotten about the drunk, still laying at the base of the bar, at Listings' feet. It seemed like the ridiculous spat with him had happened a lifetime ago. Now his attention went back to the man, if only for a moment. The big guy groaned as the music started again.

The man who held Listings hostage laughed. The same laugh Evan had heard on the phone before, the same laugh that had been pulling his brain apart, pulling apart his memories and laying him bare.

"I really don't think he likes this tune," said the madman. Then, to the drunk, he said, "I've been watching you, Ken. You're a rude pig."

The madman moved. He was fast. Faster than

Listings, and also… something else. Something more.

Something that terrified Evan.

The man's foot moved. The drunk – Ken – screamed, a single shouted "NO!" that was still too slow and then there was a nauseating crunch that was *not* bone breaking.

The madman moved back, and now the drunk was clawing at his throat. The downed man's mouth opened and closed, opened and closed, but no sound came out. Just a high-pitched whistle that made Evan's skin writhe.

He stepped toward the drunk, knowing he had to do something, not know what that could be.

And Listings seized the moment. She spun away from the madman, a blur as she moved out of range. The man slashed out, his knife seeking her neck, but she seemed to flow under it, grabbing her throat, blood around her fingers.

She came to her knees next to Evan.

"Listings!"

"I'm okay," she gasped. "Just a scratch. Look out!"

Evan wasn't *Listings*-fast, but he did all right. And in this case he was glad because it saved him from being gutted. The madman had followed Listings as she rolled, and now he slashed at Evan, who moved away in time to avoid evisceration but not fast enough to completely escape injury. Heat seared across his stomach and he heard his shirt rip. Blood rolled over the waist of his pants.

He knew the instant it happened that the cut wasn't life-threatening. Maybe he'd need stitches, but that was it.

In the same moment, he was pulling the trigger. Not realizing he was doing it, just acting on instinct. If he'd had a pillow in his hand he probably would have thrown it, but he had the gun so he pulled the trigger.

Once.

Twice.

Three times.

He was moving when he squeezed off the shots. Dodging the madman's attack, moving out of range of the knife. But even with that movement, he knew he hit what he was aiming at. He saw the front sight and rear sight line up perfectly, saw them both merge with the too-close center mass of the madman's chest in his black coat.

The three shots blasted louder than thunder in the contained space. Evan's ears rang, and he figured he'd earned himself a year of deafness as an old geezer.

He didn't care. Because all three bullets hit. He knew it. The madman who had tried to hurt Listings had been blown right out the open door of the bar.

Evan spun to Listings. She was on her knees, feeling at her neck. Blood sluiced from the long shallow gash along the left side of her neck.

"Didja get him?" she said. She was looking at the drunk.

Evan followed her gaze. The drunk – who, if madmen in trenchcoats were to be believed, had been named Ken – was staring up at the ceiling of the bar. He wasn't moving. Nor would he. One hand clutched as his throat, the other had fallen onto his crotch, as though even in death he was determined to go out as crudely as possible.

"Yeah," said Evan.

"You sure?" said Listings.

"Yeah."

She stood. Walked toward the entrance.

"Where you going?"

"I want to know who this nutcase was. And what he had to do with your wife."

They left the bar. And as they did, Evan thought, strangely, that they were moving into a darkness that would never end.

Listings pulled out her gun as they hit the street.

"You sure that you're sure?" she said.

Evan felt like he had just fallen into some funhouse mirror version of reality where cause and effect no longer ruled; where up was down and in was out and when you shot a man three times in the chest he didn't die.

There was no body on the sidewalk, no body on the street.

A man who had been shot three times, a man who should be bleeding – or dead – on the street... was nowhere to be seen.

MYSTERY

"I hit him," Evan said. He looked at the sidewalk. There was no blood there. No nothing. "Blood should be here. *He* should be here."

Listings looked up and down the street. There wasn't much to be seen. It was the middle of the night, and there wasn't a car or a person in sight. Their only company was a few moths fluttering around the flickering lights of the few streetlights that hadn't been shot out in this crappy part of town.

"You take east," she said. "I'll take west."

"Wait," said Evan. "We shouldn't –"

But his partner was already moving off, and was half a block away before he could sufficiently gather his thoughts to do anything.

"Dammit, Listings." He shouted, "Call it in!"

"Fine!"

She kept moving, but he knew she'd call it in. She couldn't be controlled, but at times she could be directed. Like a wild horse that refused to be broken, but occasionally consented to let someone ride her. They had had a tough time in the beginning of their partnership, until Evan finally managed to break through her tough-as-nails exterior, through the tough-as-*tougher*-nails *interior*, and find what was at the center. What she was made of. She was about justice. About righting wrongs, about finding evil and punishing it. And the dozens of partners she'd gone through just hadn't known how to deal with that, how to yield to her and yet keep her as a part of their lives, a part of their partnership.

Evan had figured it out, eventually. He still wasn't sure how. But what they had worked. He didn't know what he'd do without Listings, and hoped she felt the same about him. That he mattered, that he made her better.

For a second he saw the knife at her throat again. Saw how close she had come to just… *ending*. For a second he saw Val's face next to Listings', and saw both of them dying. Dying, then living, then dying, then living. On and on forever, with him watching, him suffering.

Evan tried to pull himself away from that thought by looking around. But he didn't like what he was seeing. Didn't like that he had come here and found himself twisting in some kind of setup, had shot a man point-blank and the man hadn't died. Even with a bullet-proof vest, three shots at that range should have broken his ribs, maybe knocked him unconscious.

And Evan didn't think the guy – the killer – had been wearing a vest.

How do you know? He could have been wearing a robot suit under that coat.

But even his own voice in his mind sounded false. No, the killer *hadn't* been wearing a vest.

So where was he? Where was the killer's body?

Evan should be looking at a dead man right now.

He glanced westward. He could barely see Listings.

He sighed, and moved east. He didn't expect to find anything, but knew that he should go at least to the end of the block. What if the psycho was propped up behind some mailbox, bleeding out and just waiting for a late-night stroller to come by so he could have a last chance to stab someone?

Though chances are in this neighborhood anyone out strolling probably deserves the stab.

The street was largely dark. All the businesses he could see were shuttered, brown roll-down storefronts splattered with graffiti and gang tags. Some of the cheaper – or poorer – business owners opted instead to leave their storefronts open to the night air. Evan suspected they were probably selling drugs or involved in other activities that required an open door at night.

"How long will we play, Evan?"

Evan froze. He turned. To his left was a dark alley, a forbidding chasm with tall walls that disappeared into a pitch black eternity. And he had just heard the voice of the killer, the words of a man who should be dead but who sounded not merely whole but *amused*. As if all this was part of the game he had arranged for them to play.

"Listings," said Evan. He whisper/yelled it, hoping against hope that his partner might be nearby. He pulled out his cell and dialed. The call went to Listings' voice mail.

The smart thing would be to wait. Wait until Listings came back, or even better call for backup and go in with a squad of guys who were all armed to the teeth. If the killer got away, well, that happened sometimes when you played it safe.

Only Evan couldn't do that. Because this wasn't just a man, wasn't just a killer. He had something to do with Val's death. And Evan had to know what.

He moved into the alley.

His eyes had adjusted to the dim light of the bar. Had adjusted further to the lesser light of the street. Now they struggled to find a way to pierce the black hole that enveloped all just a few feet off the street. The walls went up forever, disappearing into night, gray-white graffiti tattooed angrily onto them as high as the taggers could reach.

"I never would have killed anyone if I'd known this would happen, Evan," said the killer.

Evan spun. The voice seemed to come from everywhere, from his right and left side, from his own mind.

He wondered if he was going crazy. If Val's death, if not knowing what came next had been too much. Maybe he was *already* insane. Insane and hearing voices inside his head, coming from all around and surrounding him.

And, mostly, coming from farther down the alley.

He kept walking.

He could make out a few grays, shapes that at first seemed cut out of fog but that he could vaguely see were pallets and boards and boxes and trash. They were big enough for him to see, big enough that when he saw something out of the corner of his eye it scared him. He kept thinking he saw movement. But whenever he turned to face it, there was just another spray-painted shape on the wall, or a broken board leaning against a mangled box.

"But now we're locked into this game," said the killer.

Evan kept moving forward. He didn't know what was happening, exactly. Didn't know how the killer was doing this, or what he was up to, but he felt like he had no choice but to continue onward. To do otherwise would be to admit he had fallen into a world of madness, or to relinquish his own autonomy.

I walk forward because I wish to walk forward. Maybe I do

the same thing over and over, maybe I do things that make no sense. But they are my choices, and that makes it bearable.

Evan realized the words in his mind were becoming almost a chant, a prayer to combat the fear he was feeling. He kept moving forward, gun clenched in a hand that was slick with fear-sweat. But he wanted to stop. Wanted to run screaming from the alley. Wanted to forget this had ever happened. Even – especially – if it meant forgetting what the killer had to do with Val.

"Ring 'round the rosey, then ashes to ashes we all fall down."

Evan cocked his gun. "Come on out," he said. "We'll end the game."

The killer laughed that mad laugh. Evan's brain peeled apart, his mind fractured a bit. He wondered if insanity was a contagious disease. He thought it might be.

"If only I could," said the disembodied voice of a man who should be dead.

A light flashed just behind Evan, and he twisted. Leading with his gun, expecting to see the dead-mad eyes of a killer behind him.

Instead, he was greeted by the slight form of a young woman. She stood framed in an open door, pale yellow light flowing around her, bouncing off her hair.

It was the girl from the bar. Rainbow Hair.

From the front, she was just as exotic as she was from behind. Her skin was lightly tanned, with traces of freckling. Her ears were pierced four or five times each, and she had a stud in her left nostril, and two bars pierced her left eyebrow. A ring curved around her lower lip. Large, almond-shaped eyes stared at the gun that Evan was pointing at her, though she didn't seem particularly scared by it. She looked like she was probably Cambodian, maybe Vietnamese.

"Geez," said Evan, pointing the gun skyward and thanking whatever angels were watching over him that he hadn't pulled the trigger.

The young woman blinked. Her eyes widened a bit in recognition. "You," she said. Then the eyes squinted in disdain. "Bad mojo, man."

Evan wasn't sure how to take that. No one seemed to be reacting the way they should tonight. The drunk hadn't left them alone, the bullets hadn't killed the crazy, and now the girl in the alley in the middle of the night seemed totally unconcerned about the strange man with the gun.

"Did you see someone go by here?" he said. It was as much a kneejerk reaction as a well-thought question, as though he had lapsed into rote copsmanship when faced with one too many ridiculous moments in an evening determined to throw logic to the wind.

The woman shook her head. "Did *you*?"

Evan had to resist the urge to gawk at her. What was *that* supposed to mean?

"Close that door," he said gruffly. "Get inside and stay inside."

He turned back to face deeper into the alley. The spot between his shoulder blades itched, as though he half-expected the punk woman to stab him instead of retreating to safety.

She didn't stab him. But she didn't go inside, either. At least, not that he heard. The light stayed on behind him, and silence reigned in the alley.

Silence, and darkness. The light from whatever store the woman had come out of wasn't very strong, and within a few feet he had returned to the depths of the alley's abyssal reaches. Darkness, deep and black. He felt utterly isolated. But not alone. No more than a rat in a maze is alone as it is forced to walk through unending passages that spin around and in on themselves, knowing that some floors are electrocuted, some lead to food. But always it will do the same thing again, over and over, under the watchful eyes of the maze-makers, until it fails and dies.

Evan was isolated, under glass. But not alone, no. *Watched.* Watched in the deep darkness that was everywhere, in the black alley…

… that ended in a sheer wall.

The two buildings that formed the walls on either side of him apparently connected directly to the backside of another, larger building, creating a dead end at the back of the alley. The wall ahead went straight up, and Evan saw no doors or windows or even a fire escape within reach.

So where had the voice come from?

Where had the killer gone?

Was any of it real?

For a moment he saw Val's face, staring up at nothing. He saw his wife's eyes, blank and glassy and flecked with blood, and wondered if he might still be in that room. Maybe the maze he felt himself in was just a construct of his mind. Perhaps he was not really *here*, but *there*. Perhaps perception was a lie, and reality was love and blood and death and a man lost within them.

But no. He remembered too well the sound of the madman's voice on the phone, laughing as he taunted Evan about his murdered wife.

Evan wasn't insane. Or at the very least, if he was, he was the kind of insane that still lives in reality. He wasn't locked in a white room somewhere. He was here in this place, now.

Evan looked around. There were a few back doors that emptied into the alley, many of them covered by security gates, others wrapped with chains. No way the killer could have gotten through.

No way out of here. Not unless he had flown.

Or unless Evan had imagined everything.

He walked out of the alley. His gun was still in hand, and if anything he went even slower on the way out. Looking for something he might have missed, trying to find a way the killer could have lured him down here, then gotten out.

He saw nothing.

The bits of trash were still too small to hide under or behind. The doors were all shut and locked – even the one the punk girl had come out of was now locked, as grim and unyielding as every other way in or out of this passageway.

Evan tried every door on the way out. Every door was locked. They all felt cold, most of them moist with the condensation of a cool night. No one had touched them.

The killer was not here.

He had called Evan from in here. The voice had been real. But then... he had just disappeared.

"How do you kill a man who's already dead?"

Evan heard the words, and didn't know if he was hearing something real, or just remembering what had been said before. The only thing he knew, without doubt or confusion, was that he was very, very afraid.

MYSTIX

When Evan finally emerged from the alley he felt like he had come out of a dark wilderness. Like a prophet of Old Testament times, an ancient seer who had descended to the gates of some netherworld and now was returning to tell what he had observed.

Only Evan wasn't sure what he had seen. Or heard. With every step he took back into the street, the voice that had sounded so close to him seemed to drift further away. Rationalization – the grown-up equivalent of a blanket pulled up high so the monsters can't get you on the darkest nights – started to rear its head.

Maybe I didn't hear it.

A step into the street.

Maybe I heard it, but it wasn't real.

Another step.

Someone tried to kill Listings. I discharged my weapon. People's minds get weird on them when that kind of stuff happens.

A final step.

I imagined it. I must have.

Fewer than a third of the street lights were still operating here, but they seemed brighter than the sun for a moment. If he had owned sunglasses, Evan suspected he would have been tempted to put them on. He felt normal, like emerging from that dark slit had been enough to put the craziness, the *impossibility*, of the night aside for a moment.

The feeling disappeared, though, when he heard the

killer's voice again. It didn't sound like it was coming from his mind. In a way, that would have actually been comforting – every cop knows, or at least hears about, men and women who lose it working one of the hardest jobs in the world. So to start hearing voices rattling around in his skull, to see gremlins tearing at the wings of his brain-plane, would have been something he could have coped with on some level. In our enlightened age, even madness makes a certain kind of sense: once it has a name, it can be manipulated, controlled, conquered. Even if that name is insanity.

But Evan had no name for what happened as he stood under the uneven yellow light of a streetlamp. Standing there, almost gasping from some unnamed and perhaps unnamable fear, and he heard the voice.

"I'm going to kill you forever, White."

The voice was the same. A normal voice, pleasant even. The kind of voice that usually says "Have a nice day" or "You take care now" or "Drive safely, neighbor!" or any of a million other pleasantries that wrap us in a safe cocoon of non-essential communications. But it wasn't saying those things now.

"I'm going to kill you forever, White."

It wasn't in his mind. It wasn't anything as simple as madness, as one more cop who's lost his marbles after seeing one too many innocents hurt and one too many bad guys get away with it.

No, the voice came in his ear. His *right* ear. It had location, it had direction. The words were almost whispered. Like the killer was close enough to lean in and smile as he said the words. A joke between friends. Only this joke would end in blood and death.

29

Evan spun, his gun pointing the way to…

… nothing.

He whipped around, turning the other way.

Stifled a scream when he saw a form staring at him from one of the shadowed areas of the street. Then the figure moved, and as it did he knew he wasn't looking at his quarry. He knew that walk as well as he did his own.

"Wow, White," said Listings. Her own gun was out as well, but she looked relaxed. Just a jaunt in a horrific part of town in the dead of night looking for a man who tried to kill her moments before. Situation normal for her. Her hair was mussed, but even that just added to her allure, to the sense that she rolled out of bed looking like this, to the fact that with her what you saw was actually what you got. "Jumpy much?"

Evan turned and looked behind him. Back into the alley. It beckoned, the darkness both repulsive and alluring. He felt he was being pulled into something he didn't understand, couldn't handle.

Couldn't escape.

He didn't realize he had actually taken a step toward the alley until he felt Listings' hand on his arm, jerking him back to the here and now.

"Was it him?" she asked.

Evan stared into the black mouth of the alley. No longer hypnotizing him, at least not with his partner's warm hand on his arm. But still calling. The dark, the black beckoning.

He knew what she was asking. Not simply, "Did you see him in there?" although that was part of it.

No, she was asking other questions. Bigger questions. She wanted to know if Evan had recognized the man. If he had seen him before, if the killer was someone that Evan could link to what had happened to Val.

He thought for a moment. Still staring at the alley, silently willing answers forth.

Nothing came. Nothing ever comes out of darkness. Darkness is a destructive force, the thing that happens when light has expended itself, when photons die. Things don't answer from death. Only silence can be found. Only cold.

Evan finally exhaled a long breath. "I don't know," he said. "Maybe. Maybe not. I don't know." He shrugged. Tried to shed the mantle of confusion that had wrapped itself around him. It didn't work. "Regardless, he got away."

Listings looked up and down the street. "Damned if I know how."

"Yeah," said Evan.

He realized he had taken another step toward the alley. He didn't know why. Maybe he hoped that if he looked again, he might find something this time. Maybe he hoped that if he went there he would simply settle into the darkness and cease to be.

Neither would happen. And both were far too alluring. So he forced himself to turn away. Turned to his right, toward the end of the small block.

"Where you going?" said Listings.

"There was a girl I bumped into in there," said Evan, jerking a thumb over his shoulder at the alley. "She worked at a shop that should front around the corner here. Maybe she saw something."

He walked away, not waiting to see if Listings would

follow. Listings did what she wanted, she always had. But this time, whether she wanted or not, he had to find out what was going on.

Had to understand how a man could walk away from three shots in the chest.

Had to understand how a killer could speak without being seen.

Had to understand how this connected with Val. With his wife, and with her final smile.

He walked away, and pretended not to hear the voice that said, "I'll kill you. All of you. Forever." It wasn't in his ear this time, but in his mind. At least, he assumed so, because when he glanced at Listings she seemed as unconcerned as always. She hadn't heard it.

What's going on?

He had no answers for himself.

Around the corner, and it was clear where the girl had come from. This street was as dark as the one they had just left, lined with the same hunching rows of stolid, sealed businesses.

Except one. Light blazed out of one of the storefronts. It was mostly neon, yellows and blues that let the world know this place was open for business, but couldn't manage to convey any warmth with the announcement. There was a seediness to the light, almost a malaise.

As they approached he saw the name of the shop in sweeping neon letters: *Mystix*. The sign itself was leaning against the store front, plugged in with a long green extension cord that went in through the open doorway.

The other signs on the storefront were a mix of English

and what Evan recognized as Vietnamese, though he had no clue what they said. Could be "Grocery Store" or "Crack Den" or "We Kill White Police" for all he knew.

The signs in English were for a strange mix of items: a tattered ad for Bibles that looked like it had been saved from the 1960s, a computer printout on the healing power of crystals, a large picture offering frogs for sale.

"What the hell?" said Listings.

Evan shrugged.

Listings pulled out her phone. "I'm going to secure the bar."

"You didn't call yet?" Evan was irritated, but not surprised.

"I'm doing it now. You got this?"

Evan sighed. Nodded. She smiled at him, and it was a different smile than the one she used with the drunk at the bar. Not a mayhem-smile. A real one. They were rare.

It made Evan feel warm. It was a treasure, to be valued. He had been her partner for a year before he saw her smile even once. Even now, even with the way things had recently changed between them, the smiles were few and far between.

"I got this."

"You know we're in deep shit, right?"

"Yeah."

She started talking into the phone, half-running back to the bar. They hadn't exactly followed normal protocols tonight, but Evan didn't know if there were regs that really covered a surprise attack by a lunatic that turned into a chase down a street trying to find some guy who could take bullets without blinking and disappear like smoke.

Writing the report was going to be a bitch.

Listings was gone in a moment, and Evan turned back to the lit shop. The door was open, some kind of hanging made of woven bamboo strips obscuring the inside of the place. He pushed through it.

The inside of the shop was as strange and eclectic as the outside. More neon, with beads hanging everywhere. Crystals and quartzes cluttered shelves at concentrations unseen by any but the most able spelunkers.

A lot of the walls – even the ceiling – had signs as well. Some Vietnamese, some English.

There were plants in one corner. Leafy green things that each had their own dull pot, and seemed somehow angry to be trapped in the room.

Another area had bottles – what looked like entrails, chicken feet, sundry other biological materials he could only guess at.

Bibles, crosses, flasks marked with crucifixion designs sat in another area.

The air was hazy, with a vaguely herbal scent. Smoking paraphernalia was probably sold here as well, and Evan figured this must be some kind of New Age/religious/sorcery one-stop-shop.

Two women – both plump, both Vietnamese, both on the far side of seventy years old – passed him, moving toward the doorway as he came in. As they did, a shrill voice caught his attention. He turned and saw Rainbow Hair. She was sitting behind a cash register that sat on a simple stool – which he suspected would be an open entry to rip this place off every night if it weren't for the weird, almost creepy vibe the shop gave off – waving a nail polish brush in one hand

and holding the other up to dry as she shouted.

The words were in Vietnamese, so he had no idea of the details, but it wasn't hard to tell from the tone that she was irritated with the two old broads.

Evan moved to Rainbow Hair and waited for her rant to die down. She kept it going well past the time when the customers had left, though he wasn't sure if that was because she was *that* angry or just because she was trying to avoid dealing with him. He suspected the former: he didn't get a "worried about dealing with people" vibe off her. Most of the people Evan had met from southeast Asian countries were still fairly traditional in dress and grooming. Which meant they were still connected to their past, to their elders. They still had respect, they still knew what manners were.

That was changing with the young people, just as young people changed things in every culture. But to see one so radically pierced and with hair like this girl's... he suspected she had a chip on her shoulder, and one she would be only too glad to display.

"Problems with the customers?" he said.

She blew on her nails. "They never buy anything from me. Just come in and browse."

"People do that."

The young woman – and now Evan saw she was even younger than he had first thought, maybe as young as eighteen or nineteen – frowned. "It doesn't pay the bills."

"Aren't you supposed to respect your elders?"

She switched to painting the nails of her other hand. Dismissive. "Aren't *you* supposed to present a warrant?"

Evan smiled tightly. So many people – especially in neighborhoods like this – tended to think of police officers as the enemy. And it became a self-fulfilling prophecy a lot of the time. She was closing him out, so there wasn't a lot of friendly chatting they could do. But he still needed to talk to her, so....

"I'm just asking friendly questions right now. No arrests, no searches." He sniffed the hazy air loudly. Made a show of sampling it, wrinkling his nose a bit before sniffing again. "I'm sure I could arrange for one, though, if you want."

He let that hang there. Not wanting to make an adversary of this girl, but wanting her to understand he wasn't going to leave and she wasn't in a position to make him go away.

She kept painting her nails, which he expected. She wouldn't acknowledge him right away. She'd keep going for a moment, would show she was brave and that it didn't really matter what he said. But eventually –

"I told you already: I didn't see anyone in the alley."

"What were you doing out there?"

"Taking out some trash."

"Could anyone have come in when you went out?"

The girl's nose wrinkled. She looked disgusted that he would insult her with such a question. "This look like a neighborhood where you live long letting that happen?"

Evan nodded, both because she was absolutely right on that count and because he wanted her to know she had scored on him. It might make her feel more confident, might make her a bit more friendly. A lot of folks didn't realize that the person that is in charge – or thinks she is – tends to talk more. So Evan never minded looking weak or silly if it made the people he was interviewing feel a bit stronger, a bit bigger... a bit more chatty.

"What were you doing in the bar earlier?" he said.

The girl looked at him again, this time rewarding his question with a gaze that he suspected she reserved for the truly stupid people in her life. "Borrowing a book," she said.

"What about the store?"

"What about it?"

"Anyone weird come in tonight?"

She laughed, a short but melodious laugh that made her seem a bit softer. "Everyone who comes in here is weird."

Evan sighed. "You don't like me much, do you?" When all else fails, he thought, try just saying what's on everyone's mind.

The store was lit by low-watt overhead fluorescents. When he said this they flickered, as though in agreement. The girl noticed. She made a sign with her right hand, a movement that he probably would have thought was a gang sign under other circumstances. With this girl, however, he knew it was something else. Nothing so terrestrial as a shout-out to some crew, though perhaps more dangerous. A warding, a spell. Perhaps a curse.

"I told you," she said. "You got bad mojo."

At that moment Evan was struck by a sense of déjà vu. Not just at her wording, but something about this place seemed familiar. He'd never worked this part of the city before, so he'd never been on this street that he could remember.

But he felt like –

"What?" said the girl. He must have zoned out or been staring at her oddly, because the word didn't mean "What did you say?" but rather "What the hell is wrong with you?"

Evan snapped out of the moment. "Have I seen you before?" he said.

"The bar. Duh." She painted her pinky nail. Started waving that hand around and blowing on it. The nails were beautifully done. She'd have a career as a manicurist if that was a good sample of her work.

"No. I mean...." He sighed, not sure how to end that sentence. "Forget it. What's your name?"

"Tuyen," she said.

"That's pretty. Is that a first or a last name?"

She stared at him, and he could tell now that he'd gone too far. She wasn't going to be buttered up and she wasn't going to talk to some strange white cop about anything more than she had to.

"Do you have security tapes here?"

"No." Her voice was even frostier now. She was tired of him, she wanted him gone.

He chuckled and pointed to the corner of the store behind her. A closed-circuit camera swiveled slowly back and forth above a cluster of Virgin Mary statues. "Why don't I believe you?"

Tuyen stared at him blankly, and he could practically hear her calculating whether he would give up and go away if she kept being difficult or if it would be faster just to deal with him.

She finally got up and walked toward the back wall. Evan followed. The back wall was covered top to bottom by a long black curtain. Tuyen shivered as she stopped at the thick drapery.

"Someone walk on your grave?" said Evan.

"I hate it back here."

"Not your style?"

She threw that disgusted look at him again. "I'm not Hmong."

She parted the curtain in the middle and stepped through.

Evan did the same, and realized that the curtain wasn't covering a back wall, but instead bisected the store neatly in half. He also understood why Tuyen had shivered, and had to resist an urge to do the same.

The back half of Mystix was dark. Not pitch black, but the lights were lower here. There was shelving, same as in the front, but the shelves seemed older, less stable. As though the owner of the store – whether that was Tuyen or someone else – had never bothered with any upkeep back here.

And what was on the shelves was the kind of thing Evan didn't understand. He could conceptualize what he was seeing, but not its uses. Not its reasons.

He saw chopsticks, lashed together in inverted crosses, each with the dried body of a gutted lizard lashed to it. Beside them was a spot on the floor with no shelves, but piled high with a variety of animal skulls.

The back wall – the real back wall – of the store drew his attention most of all. There were a trio of animals, what he guessed were creatures indigenous to Vietnam, stuffed and mounted on the otherwise empty space. A five-foot-long python with blood-red scales, a snub-nose monkey with a bluish face, and the shriveled body of something that looked like a baby jackal or maybe a small dog.

The python's jaws were unhinged, stretched wide, and

it had swallowed half the monkey, which was around three feet long. The monkey had been arranged to look in agony, its arms splayed and its back arched. But at the same time it was busy chewing the baby jackal. And the jackal in turn had the tail of the python lodged deep in its throat.

The things were devouring each other forever, a horrifically conceived murder-suicide as each beast killed a foe and in so doing also swallowed the world of its own existence.

Evan had been on the force almost twenty years. He had seen murder, rape, torture, abuse – so much so that it all tended to blend sometimes; it all tended to seem like the same thing over and over again. But this circle of endless death sent chill-spasms up and down his back in a way few things did anymore.

"Jesus," he whispered.

"He's not here," said Tuyen. Her voice was low. Lost in a shadowland between reverence and fear.

The animals' eyes were sewn shut. And as soon as he saw that, the interpretation of the circle changed. Now they seemed to be vomiting, to be giving violent birth to one another, to the things that would eventually kill them.

Either way, death.

Evan looked at the curtain. It was the thing farthest away from the gruesome death-circle, and he didn't want to see those animals right now. Or ever again.

Tuyen saw him staring at the cloth. "Some Hmong believe the spirits can't pass through doors. They can appear anywhere, but places with no doors invite them."

That made it all worse somehow: the idea that there

was no place safe, but that *this* place had been designed to specifically lure things from the other side.

Evan sensed movement. He turned toward it, and saw a large shape among the shelves at the back. Someone lurking. Perhaps a shopper, perhaps just another chubby old lady – albeit one interested in a darker sort of magic than the jolly-seeming women he had seen earlier.

Still, his fingers itched. He wanted to grab his gun. Wanted to just start shooting.

"Don't worry about him," said Tuyen. "Come on."

She pulled Evan's sleeve, almost yanking him along. Normally he wouldn't care to have a comparative stranger pulling him around in a dark voodoo shop, but he was grateful for her touch. It grounded him, the warmth of her hand even through his coat seeming to remind him that reality still had at least a toehold in his existence.

He moved with her to the back of the dark section. There was an open door there, which admitted them to a coffin of a room. No windows, just a desk, a chair, a small filing cabinet, a computer. Above the desk a small cabinet had been built into the wall. And that was it. No pictures, no other ornamentation. The small business office of a person who either made little money or whose main business was not in bookkeeping but in people. Perhaps both.

A small gooseneck lamp cast a weak cone of light over the desk, cutting the computer keyboard into zones of light and dark. It flickered, an exhausted beam of light that needed tending. Tuyen tapped it impatiently and cursed in Vietnamese.

She opened the cabinet above the computer. Inside was a small closed-circuit video setup. Not much, basically just a foot-square monitor with an attached video recorder. Evan had seen thousands of them. This looked like a cheap model, the kind designed to record, then automatically rewind and record again so that the owner would have a record of whatever happened in the last two or six hours, but nothing else.

The monitor was dark. Gray-green and strangely unsettling when it was revealed, like the eye of a sleeping demon that had yet to be awakened.

Tuyen flicked a red switch at the base of the machine and a pin of light appeared in the monitor. An instant later it widened to encompass the entire screen. The image flashed and flared, a gray/green/black/white mélange of motion. The lines were oddly hypnotic, and Evan found himself staring at the monitor, falling into it.

It was a view of the front of the shop, he finally realized. But a distorted view, as if someone had pulled reality like taffy and then shredded the results before gluing it all together in a lunatic hodge-podge.

The effect was creepy. Disturbing. And somehow beautiful as well. As if Evan might find all the answers he wanted and needed if he could only find a way to see behind the distortions.

"What's this?" he finally managed. His voice sounded like it was coming from someone else.

Tuyen sounded strangely distant, too. "I told you we don't have tapes," she said. "Or at least, none that are worth anything."

She whacked the side of the monitor. The sound hit Evan like a gunshot, like –

(the vision of his dead wife)

42

– a bolt of lightning, shocking him at least partially back to reality.

The blurred image on the screen shimmied under the blow, then returned. Evan looked away before it caught his attention again. Trying to convince himself that the sweat he felt trickling down his neck and armpits was just because he was concentrating, not because he was suddenly terrified.

"Stupid thing's been broken forever," said Tuyen. She sounded enraged, seething. And Evan had been a cop long enough – which meant he had been studying people long enough – to see that she was using rage to mask fear.

Tuyen was terrified of this monitor.

"It's still running tape, though?" he said.

She shrugged. "Sure. Maybe. Depends on if the day shift guy put one in last time it was working."

She pressed a button on the machine. Something deep in the base of the thing grinded resentfully, then a motor hummed with only slightly less attitude. The gray plastic cover under the monitor flicked back and a black video tape spit out.

"You're in luck," said Tuyen. She pulled the tape out and turned to Evan.

"You gonna put a new one back in?"

"Why bother?" She nodded at the monitor, which still showed a spliced mess of the world.

She handed the tape to Evan and he reached to take it. Their fingers brushed for just a second.

The tiny office was closeted, and it was a dry night. Static must have built up in their bodies, because when he touched her there was a sharp jolt at his fingers. Unusually strong for a static shock, but still the sort of thing you just ignored in polite company.

Tuyen apparently missed the "How To Ignore Shocks, Farts, and Burps" class at her finishing school. She gasped and stepped back so fast she almost collided with the desk. Evan reached out to steady her and she did a sort of epileptic limbo to avoid his hand.

"What?" he said. He was worried, but also annoyed. It was a shock, he'd felt it, too. So he knew it wasn't worth this kind of response. "You okay?" he said, and hoped he sounded sincere instead of just irritated.

Tuyen didn't answer. She looked at the monitor, and straightened without ever taking her eyes off it. Evan didn't look at it, telling himself it was because she was acting weird and he didn't want to take his eyes off *her*, though he knew that was only partly true.

He didn't want to look at that screen again. And realized that he was less afraid of seeing the strangely beautiful distortions than he was of seeing what they might reveal if they suddenly disappeared.

What is *reality tonight?*

"You need to throw that tape away," said Tuyen.

"What?"

"Forget whatever you're doing."

"I'm a cop, Tuyen. I can't just 'forget' stuff."

"Sure you can. Cops do it all the time. I've seen it."

She was still holding the tape. She hadn't let go when she pulled away from him, she had yanked it out of his hand. Evan reached for it. Took it gingerly by a corner, being careful not to touch her again so she wouldn't go crazy and tell him –

(what she saw)

– a bunch of crazy hooey about Vietnamese smoke monsters or something.

He tried to take the tape. She didn't release it.

"Let go of what you're doing," she said. "Whatever you find, it won't bring happiness."

Evan yanked the tape out of her fingers. He dug a card out of his pocket and handed it to her. She took it like it was a venomous slug – something dangerous and disgusting.

"Call me if you think of anything you want to talk to me about," he said.

She didn't answer.

He was glad. He told himself it was because he'd had enough of her particular brand of crazy for the night.

But deep inside, in that place where we cannot lie – not even to the one person most likely to believe our lies, which is to say ourselves – he knew that he didn't want to hear her speak because she knew more than she had let on. And the things she hadn't said might very well destroy him.

SHADOWS

Tuyen was a child of more than one world.

She wasn't one of those who remained hide-bound to the "old ways," as if it would be a good thing to someday return to rice farming and a mortality rate that hadn't changed much for hundreds of years. But neither was she one of her many friends who had completely divested themselves of what it meant to be Vietnamese and seemed bent on proving they could kill themselves with cheeseburgers and porn as fast as any other "real" American.

She liked to dress in jeans and t-shirts because they were cute. She dyed her hair and had piercings because she thought they looked good, even though her mother and grandmother had both muttered about them until the day they died.

But she *was* Vietnamese. She loved the stories her grandmother had told, loved the food her mother had taught her to cook. She was a bit of both – old and new – and she figured that was the best way to be.

One of the things she *didn't* like about the old ways was the almost manic superstition that some people brought with them; the clinging, cringing terror of ghosts and demons and devils and spirits.

But she liked even less the attitude of so many Americans – the attitude that only what they saw was real, and then only if it could be poked, prodded, destroyed, and then reproduced for further testing. Tuyen wouldn't allow herself to be dominated in every moment by a terror of unknown forces, but she *did* know that some things existed beyond the pale of human control, some situations resisted "rational" understanding.

And she felt like she was in one of those situations now.

She could tell that Detective Evan White according to the card he had left behind was one of the people who demanded proof. Who wouldn't believe in a demon if it came and possessed his own mother – not unless that demon returned at a predetermined time and place to possess a second person as proof that the first time hadn't been a fluke.

But Tuyen did believe. She had to. She saw things. She saw the truth of things. Not always, thank God. Truth was something that so many people claimed to want, but really truth was something that almost no one could handle. Too much truth would damage anyone. Too much truth could kill. Or worse.

She had sensed evil clinging to White when she touched his hand. Sensed darkness clutching at him, pulling him toward her.

Some of that darkness she knew. Some of it she understood. Some of it was unfamiliar to her, and she did not understand it. She did not want to, either.

She had seen White before, of course – at least in pictures. But it had been a shock to see him in here, in the shop. Not a picture but a living, breathing person.

She had thought she was past that. She had thought that part of her life had ended.

She looked at the monitor that still showed the security feed. It writhed in and around and over itself like a serpent, or like worms through the rotted flesh of life.

A shadow passed over the monitor. A momentary darkening that passed from left to right, then disappeared. Tuyen gasped, turned her head to see if anyone had come into the room.

No. She was alone. And even if someone *had* entered, there was no way that anyone could have thrown a shadow like that. The lighting in here was wrong for it.

She looked back at the monitor. Leaned in close, closer, peering into the dissolution that rampaged across the screen, trying to understand, to *see*.

Why was White here? He had asked if she had seen anyone, but was that really what he meant?

Was this about his wife?

White's card crumpled in Tuyen's hands as she leaned closer to the monitor.

She had always been able to see truth. Her grandmother and mother both had the gift of true-seeing. They had been fortune-tellers, revered and sought after for advice and for wisdom.

No one came to Tuyen – that was another reason she dressed and acted like she did. She loved much of her past, much of where she came from, but she did not want to live her life as a servant of people coming with the same grasping, greedy questions. Will I be rich? Will he love me? Is she cheating on me? Over and over, forever the same, always repeating and never changing.

She wanted her sight for herself, not for everyone else.

But of late her abilities had waned. The fortunes she cast were vague, barely better than the crap in the astrology section of a magazine. Her readings were murky, and the few things she did see… always dark.

She turned off the security monitor. The screen blanked, and now she was staring only at herself, the blurry outlines of a Tuyen who lived in the wraithlands on the other side of the glass.

She went back into the section of the store that was dedicated to darkness. She hated it, and the owner of the store – a wizened old man named Pham Duong – assured her he did, too. He only kept such things because the people demanded it, because the community needed darkness so that it would understand how bright the light.

That was what he said. But he had a glitter in his eyes sometimes. The things in the dark arts were costly. He made much money in the back half of the store – and money was something that both Americans and people rooted in the old ways seemed to agree on. So Pham Duong sighed, and shook his head. He whispered how much he would prefer not to have these "awful things" in his store. But then he stocked more of them, and increased the prices when he could.

The lights flickered. On, off. On, off.

Then just off.

Tuyen wrapped her arms around herself. She hurried to the curtain. She needed to leave. Needed to –

A sound stopped her. It was low. Not even a whisper. Not even a breath, almost a feeling. But it was enough. Enough to stop her, to anchor her feet to the floor.

She turned her head. Looked behind her.

The monstrosity on the back wall was dimly visible. Blood python, Tonkin snub-nose monkey, a jackal born too soon. All eating each other.

Their eyes were open.

The muscles in Tuyen's face started rippling. Her heart beat sledgehammer blows against the inside of her chest. Terror held her so tightly she couldn't breathe.

Is this real?

Is this my sight?

Is this real?

The eyes had never been opened, the things' eyes had come sewn shut. That was part of the things' magic, to know it was forever eating in ignorance, for all darkness was ignorant; all destruction was blind.

But now... each beast stared into space. Their eyes seemed to glow, and Tuyen's heart skipped as she saw that each creature had one black eye and one white. Another sign. Darkness and light, chaos in sight.

She cried out, and managed to coax her feet into movement. She ran through the curtain, into the front of the store.

The eclectic mix of magic and religion, of West and East that the store presented, usually comforted her. She had been born in the U.S., but she had been suckled on stories of Vietnam. She knew the old country as a place that had been invaded many different times by many different powers. It had always survived, not by conquering but by adapting. Catholics and Buddhists and Cao Dài could all be found, and many Vietnamese practiced bits of each religion, as well as parts of the tribal beliefs they had grown up with while cultivating rice since time untold.

But the usual comfort she found in this strange mix of belief was not here. Not now. The lights had flickered out in this part of the store as well. And again, Tuyen couldn't tell if that was what was really happening, or merely what she was *seeing*. Sometimes she saw truth, but truth did not always mirror reality. Reality was just a mask the universe wore. To teach us to see a bit at a time. To prepare us for a day when we might understand everything, and in so doing be allowed to stand with our ancestors in holy places. That was what Tuyen's grandmother had always said, and not until now had Tuyen understood what it meant.

She felt something writhe inside her. Terror.

What if she was about to see – *really* see? What if the mask was about to be ripped away, and the truth revealed?

Tuyen didn't think she could handle that.

She had been moving, pushing her way through the dark store, operating by muscle-memory, avoiding the piles of plant cuttings and relics and other paraphernalia as she moved. Now she stopped, her feet seeming to glue themselves to the floor.

Someone was here.

Someone was watching her.

She saw the form – a dark figure at the front of the store. For a moment she thought it was someone inside with her, then realized that whoever it was was just outside. Standing in the darkness beyond the window.

She couldn't make out the person's features – the window was smeared with grime and soot from the city air – but she could see what looked like the shape of a man. Not a hulk or a leviathan, nothing overtly superhuman about his form. But still, her heart began racing even faster, to the point she worried about becoming the youngest heart attack victim ever recorded.

The man just stared. His face a blur beyond the glass.

Tuyen had a sudden realization. A sudden sense of

wonder and dread.

What if this *was* about Detective White's wife? In more ways than he knew?

"Please don't hurt me." She whispered the words, so low that there was no way the man/beast/demon/thing on the other side of the glass could hear her.

The figure laughed. Low, quiet. The laugh of a man. But it chilled her to the bone, made her feel like someone was yanking her soul right out of her body.

The figure moved. Tuyen shrank back, terrified he was going to come into the store. There was nothing to stop him – the door was wide open, the bamboo hanging would not keep him away if he wanted in.

And she didn't know if iron bars or a steel door would have sufficed to keep him out.

But he turned the opposite way. His form seemed to flow, and she wondered if she was seeing a vision again. Wondered if what had happened to her grandmother at the end – she had died a wreck of a woman, drooling and screaming about spirits everywhere – would happen now to her.

She stared at the empty window a long time. The lights came back on, though she did not touch them. She did not know – and likely never would – if the darkness had been real, if it had been true, or if it had been vision.

She went to the stool with the cash register. She realized she was still holding the business card Detective White had given her, and shoved it absently in her purse.

Did this have to do with him?

With his wife?

What did the man – or spirit, or demon – at the window have to do with all this? And why had he seemed to melt?

Then she realized the man wasn't really melting or becoming something impossible.

He was just wearing a coat. A long, black coat.

It should have been a comfort. It should have made her feel better, to know she hadn't witnessed wings sprouting from the back of an animal spirit, or from an evil demon.

But it didn't. Whoever was watching her had worn a long black coat. A man, most certainly.

But some men could be demons.

CAPTAIN

The clock read 3:36 A.M.

Evan knew that, because he kept looking at it. Wondering how much longer it would be before he could sleep, knowing it was going to be far too long.

He was always tired.

Life had turned into a series of night-day-night-days that blended together. That was what death did, what grief and mourning did. He had always heard about that effect, but never experienced it. Not until Val.

Still, shouldn't it have ended by now? Shouldn't he have started healing?

Maybe not. Maybe he never would.

He supposed he should be grateful; he had known longer nights. The fact that he had run into a murderer at a bar, that a fatality had occurred, that shots had been fired – all of them added hours to his night. At least he wasn't the forensics team. They'd probably be at the bar for the better part of twenty-four hours.

And, he already knew, they'd find nothing. Or maybe too much. At a certain point, the difference between a dearth of information and a wealth of it was meaningless. If there was no evidence their hands were tied, but if there was so much information they couldn't make sense of it, that wasn't any better. And at a place like a bar in a seedy part of town, Evan doubted they'd be able to parse out the meaningful from the meaningless.

So he couldn't count on them finding anything. Couldn't count on anyone else getting this done.

If anyone was going to find out who the killer had been, it was him. He had to find out. Had to know.

"What's important is the look on your wife's face when she died." That was what the guy had said.

What did he mean? What was he trying to tell Evan? What game was he playing?

Kr-chunk.

A paper cup slipped down onto the metal grate of the vending machine. A moment later, boiling brown piss-water that was not coffee in any but the strictest technical sense started spewing out of the off-white spout above it. A few drops even landed in the cup.

Then the spout seemed to fly into a rage. Boiling, spurting flashes of coffee went everywhere. The cup fell over and long swaths of coffee dripped down the side of the machine and onto the well-stained carpet below.

Evan just stared at it for a moment. "Well, screw you very much as well," he finally managed.

He wasn't really mad. The coffee machine was old, just like everything else at the precinct building. LAPD was severely underfunded, the victim of opposing demands for greater budgetary restraint without impacting police activity levels. An impossible task, which meant that half the people in charge of the purse strings threw up their hands a long time ago and decided to let everything go to hell.

The other half – the good ones – tried to hold onto police officers and support staff. But that meant "nonessentials" – things like cars and computers and coffee machines – got older and older and fell into disrepair. And the cops still got laid off or retired.

Still, Evan had really wanted that coffee.

He stood there another moment, as though by doing so time might turn back and return the little bits of coffee to the cup. It didn't happen, so he went to the nearest door in the precinct basement. The basement was where they kept the evidence locker, some storage lockers, a (nonworking) coffee machine, and the object of his interest: the A/V room.

Through the open door, he felt like he was in high school again, going to the school library to check out a video player for Ms. Romy's history class. It was mostly dark in the room, with banks of machinery lined up haphazardly throughout the space. Along one wall was a line of library-style carrels, each with a television monitor, a DVD player, and a VCR. The televisions had headsets hanging off them for private listening, so detectives could come in and watch or listen to videos when the conference rooms weren't available or when they didn't want to watch something at their desks.

More often than not, they got used to watch rented movies by cops who were looking for an hour or two of peace after their shifts ended, some decompression time before they went home from murder and mayhem to deal with domestic chaos. Evan had never done that. He had always rushed home.

He had loved to see Val. Had loved to see her face. Her smile.

He dragged his mind away from that thought, from the vision that surfaced every time he thought of her. The blood. The unseeing terror.

The black security tape that Tuyen had given him sat on the desk at one of the carrels. Evan sat down and pushed it into the VCR. The machine turned on automatically. He pressed rewind. He considered putting on the headphones, but decided against it. He didn't remember there being any sound on the tape at Mystix, and if there was he'd just listen to it *au naturel*.

"You know it wasn't your fault."

The fact that he knew the voice didn't keep Evan from jerking, even as he smiled. "Crap on a cracker, Geist!" he shouted. He spun to face the man behind him.

Max Geist was in his mid-fifties. He'd been in the department forever, and on days when Evan felt like throwing in the towel and leaving the force for a more rewarding career as a sewage taster or someone who cleans skunk anuses, Geist was always there to remind him *why* they were there. To tell him gently that it wasn't about budgets or politics or the bad guys who got away or the good ones they couldn't help. It was about the people they *did* manage to protect. The little bits of justice they *did* bring to the world.

Evan always felt like a hypocrite, like a worthless jerk next to Geist. But he always wanted to be better after talking to the captain. So instead of quitting he came in and signed the call sheet and sat at his desk and went to work.

Tall and lean, with a hawkish nose and thin glasses that always looked like they were in danger of falling off, Geist looked more like a school teacher than a cop. But the captain's dad had been a cop, Geist's granddad had been one. It was in the man's blood. He had been doomed to this destiny from birth.

Now he smiled, a twinkle in his eyes that seemed to brighten the dim A/V room. Another reason that Evan loved the man. He was more than just a commanding officer, a boss, a mentor. He was a friend. "Sorry, White," he said.

"Didn't mean to scare you." And of course Evan could see that was exactly what he meant to do. Most cops – especially career cops – were possessed of senses of humor that veered toward the morbid. It was a defense mechanism, a way of coping with the breakdown of reality that picked away at them. So sneaking up on someone in a dark room wasn't beyond even the captain.

Hell, it *especially* wasn't beyond the captain.

Geist sat on the carrel table, squeezing his skinny backside into the space beside the VCR. "I read your report."

Evan's throat constricted. His gaze fell away from Geist's eyes.

"Hey, kid," said Geist, "I started this conversation with 'it wasn't your fault.' So don't get all guilty on me."

"I should have gone in with backup."

Geist snorted. "Gone in where? To some meeting with a crank-calling fruitcake who got your number?"

Evan looked up. Did his best to drill into Geist, letting his guilt for the bar, for the fight, for... *everything*... show as clear as he could. Hoping that someone would call him out for it. Sometimes we need to be called out. "He knew about my wife," he said.

"So does anyone who can read the *Times*," said the captain. He waved a dismissive hand. "Give yourself a break, kid." He was quiet a moment, looking introspective for a second before adding, "Though taking Listings with you was probably a mistake."

Another voice came from the darkness of the room: "I heard that."

Evan jumped again, though not as high this time. He

hoped. That mischievous twinkle in Geist's eyes doubled, though, so Evan suspected he was fooling himself: he probably jumped *higher* this time.

And in a way that was good. It was what he needed. He needed to be reminded that his friends didn't care what had happened to him. Or that they did, but it didn't change the way they felt about him. Their love for him.

Geist grinned at Listings, who was coming toward them both. "I'm glad you heard it, Listings. It would have been wasted if you hadn't."

"Is anyone else waiting in here?" said Evan, making a show of peering about what he could see of the room.

Listings ignored the question. She was pushing a cart that had a newer-model TV/VCR combo ratchet-tied to it. "Newer" meant that it had probably been invented some time after Reagan's presidency. One wheel squeaked on the cart.

She nodded at the machine he was using. "That one's crap, White," she said.

"They're all crap. The department hasn't had a working piece of equipment since before I got here." Geist chuckled at that, and Evan added, "That includes you. Sir."

Listings nodded. "Welcome to the land of eternal budget cuts." Then she jutted out her chin. "Still, this one's *less* crappy."

Geist spoke again. "Evan, back to what we were talking about: other than taking Officer Detective Miss Rambo here, nothing tonight was your fault. Mostly." He hopped off the carrel desk and clapped Evan on the back and then headed for the still-open door to the basement.

"Did you read Listings' report yet?" said Evan.

Geist shook his head, an amused grin on his face. "I

never read hers before daybreak. Too scary." He put his hands to his ears. "Too much bad language for my sweet tender ears."

Geist turned away again. Again Evan's words stopped him. He felt like a nervous parishioner, trying to get up the courage to confess to the priest. "Captain?" Geist paused at the door. "What if this is him?"

Geist thought a moment before returning to the carrel. He wasn't joking anymore: the smile was gone from his face, the twinkle had fled from his eyes. He knelt next to Evan, their faces level with one another. "I love you like a son. I've covered for you, taught you, helped you. But I've never lied to you." He paused, and Evan saw a flash of something dark and a little scary in his friend's eyes. "If this is the guy, then we'll catch him. Or kill him."

Geist turned and strode away. Gone before Evan could say another word.

Evan remained at his seat for another moment, just thinking about what the captain had said. Wondering if the man meant it: meant that he would be willing to kill the man who murdered Val, that he would be willing to kill for Evan.

He thought so. And didn't know whether that left him warm or cold inside.

He stood and went to Listings, who was waiting with something surprisingly close to patience. Or that's what he thought, until he got close enough to see the irritation flashing in her eyes.

Uh-oh.

Her fist slammed out like a steam piston. She hit him in the stomach, an upward-curving punch that completely knocked the breath out of him. His diaphragm spasmed. He couldn't breathe. Couldn't even *try*.

"Thanks for having my back there," she said, the words barely audible through gritted teeth.

Then she grabbed him.

And kissed him. Hard.

Somewhere in the middle of the kiss, Evan's muscles stopped spasming. But he still couldn't breathe. Listings had that effect on him. She always had.

He had never been unfaithful to Val. Not once, in their eleven years of marriage. But when he had been assigned to Angela Listings as a partner, he had to admit she was stunningly beautiful. It was the worst kind of beautiful, too: it was *real*. Not the kind of beauty that so many women – even Val, he had to admit to himself – aspired to, the kind of beauty that draped across magazine covers in the form of over-sexualized, hyper-posed bodies hidden under too much makeup and not enough clothing.

No, Listings was a woman who appeared to be just what she was. She wore little makeup, and rarely put on jewelry of any kind. She spoke her mind.

And she was deeply interesting.

Evan thought about asking for a transfer. He didn't have any intentions of cheating on his wife. But intentions didn't just *happen*, they were something that you had to nurture. He didn't want to put himself in a position where he found himself lusting after a woman who wasn't his wife, especially not one who was with him the majority of every day.

After a few days, he realized it wouldn't be a problem. Listings was beautiful, real, smart. She was also emotionally guarded to pathological levels. And Evan wasn't a one-night stand guy. He wouldn't fall in love with a woman who couldn't fall in love with *anyone*.

They stayed partners. And at some point they became friends. She told him about her life, about why she was a cop, why she was the *way* she was.

He was faithful to Val. Body and soul.

But when Val died....

Listings was there. She helped him get through the first days. No hint of romance. Evan wasn't allowed anywhere near the murder investigation – that was irrevocable policy, not to mention just good common sense – so she had inserted herself in the case and shepherded it as best she could for him.

And somewhere along the way, he realized that Listings' walls were down – or if not down, then at least there were breaches here and there. And as for him... Val was gone. No, not just gone: she hadn't been interested in him for a long time. He had been faithful to her, but it turned out that had not been a mutual requirement in her mind.

Listings pulled away from him, the kiss ended, and he could finally breathe again.

"I've gotta get used to the way you go off shift," he said.

"This?" She punched him again. Softer, thankfully. No bruised ribs. "This is just a coffee break." She kissed him again. The kiss was softer as well, but still passionate. It lingered long enough that Evan worried someone might come in and see them locked together. Dating a fellow officer wasn't necessarily against the rules, but dating your partner *always* was.

Still, he didn't pull away. He couldn't. He was with her now, and he couldn't draw back. That wasn't in his nature. He would stay with her.

Like you stayed with Val. And look how that turned out. Look what she did.

This is different.

As though sensing his thoughts, Listings broke the kiss. "What is it?" she said. Her eyes narrowed to slits. Everything was an extreme with her, and that was both wonderful and frustrating. No half-measures. Love, hate, joy, pain, suspicion, irritation... it was all or nothing with her, as though her heart only had room for one thing at a time.

"I...." He almost told her. Almost opened up about everything he feared, everything he felt. About his worries, his guilt. About the idea that maybe he could have stopped what happened with Val if he'd been a better husband, had been more aware of her, more aware of whatever it was that had driven her away.

The moment passed. Now he saw the killer, holding the knife to Listings' throat. Unlike his partner, he had plenty of room for different emotions. The only problem was, they were all negative: fear, guilt, loss, longing. Maybe that was why she attracted him so powerfully: she represented something he never had been, never could be, but always wished for.

"Nothing," he said.

"Talk to me, White."

Her eyes were no longer suspicious, but stubborn. She wasn't going to leave this alone. "I don't know if we should be on this one," he said. "At least, not together."

She was quiet for a second, then her brows drew

together. "Is this because of what happened to your wife?" she finally said. And without waiting for an answer, she continued, "She's been gone *forever*, White. And even before she was killed, she was cheating on you."

"I know. No, it's not that. It's...." He touched her throat. A caress. "That crazy asshole had you, Listings. He could have –"

She knocked his hand away. "Don't. You. *Dare*. You feel guilty if you've got to. But don't you stop chasing a killer because you're worried about me." She kissed him once more. She was still angry, so the kiss felt half like love, half like he was being punched again. "Or I will kick your ass faster than you can blink."

She turned to the gaping doorway, the darkness of the basement beyond beckoning like some strange netherworld that only cops working well beyond quitting time were privy to. "Now, as I was ever-so-gently reminded by you and the captain, I still have a report to write. I'll look over the CSI reports of the crime scene as they come in, too. Let you know if anything shows up." She took a step and was half in the room, half out. Then she looked at Evan and he was surprised to see an unusual expression on her face: concern. "Do *you* want to do this? Someone else could cover it."

Evan thought about it. Did he want to know? Val had proven she had her share of secrets. Did he want to know more of them? Did he want the *world* knowing them?

He nodded. "Yeah. I want to know."

Listings nodded curtly. "Good. I could never forgive myself if I found out I was sleeping with a coward."

Evan watched her go, smiling as she left. The smile felt awkward on his face. Real, because there was no doubt in his mind that he was in love with Listings. But forced, because it felt so much like he had found someone that he was destined to lose again. Maybe not in the same way he had lost Val – he would never lose Listings like that, he would *never* let something like that happen again – but the ways to suffer loss were as infinite and varied as the ways to discover joy.

Her footsteps echoed into the basement beyond the door, then disappeared. Silence took them. He felt like it was an omen, a sign. He felt like he was going to lose her. Like he had already lost her, and simply hadn't realized it yet.

Don't be an idiot.

He turned back to the carrel he was going to watch the tape on. And felt fear lurch through him.

Had he turned the TV on? He remembered putting the tape in the VCR, remembered rewinding it.

But the TV?

He must have, because it was on.

Yeah. I must have.

He sat down. Trying to ignore the fact that he didn't *remember* turning it on.

I must have.

The lines were the same as they had been at Mystix. Floating waves of randomness that came oh-so-close to forming something recognizable, then disintegrated to chaos at the last instant. They were monochromatic, but the pixels of the TV monitor seemed to have trouble with the free-floating distortions, so flashes of color kept appearing and then disappearing.

Evan watched, determined to spot something he could use. And wondering why he cared. Why he was bothering with a security tape that didn't work for a location that had no proven connection to anything that mattered.

He kept looking. Feeling like he was being guided. No, it was stronger. He felt *compelled*. Like he was playing a part in a long-running play, and if he failed to perform properly he would be not merely booed but destroyed by his unseen audience.

He sat up sharply. For a moment, the images on the screen had seemed to coalesce. Just an instant, a flash so quick he couldn't be sure if what he saw was real or imagination or just the misfiring of neurons operating on too much caffeine and too little sleep.

But it had looked like a face.

It had looked like Val.

He leaned in closer to the television.

He kept watching.

Kept playing his part.

PRAYER

Tuyen stood in her apartment, and felt – as she had felt more and more recently – like she was in a strange place. Like she didn't belong. She was not occupant, but alien.

Her grandmother was dead, and that was much of it. Gramma had been her last link to family, since Tuyen's mother had been killed in a drive-by shooting seven years before.

Tuyen was alone. The delicious smell of Gramma's *bò kho*, a beef stew with carrots and rice noodles, never greeted her when she came home from working nights at Mystix or days cleaning houses. Sometimes Tuyen left the television on so that it would be playing reruns of *General Hospital* when she got home, but knowing that Gramma wasn't watching it made the voices sound empty and hollow. The sounds of ghosts, of the dead watching the dead.

But beyond Gramma's death, beyond the fact that she had no one left, lately things had seemed... wrong. The world seemed to be adrift, as though the gravity that had so long held the universe in a series of rings within rings was finally weakening, allowing things to spin into eternity. More than once Tuyen had considered leaving. Just walking out of her apartment door, not bothering to quit her jobs, not even taking anything but the clothes on her back.

She would wander. She would be free. She wouldn't own anything, but Gramma always said owning too much just meant that many things owned *you*.

But every time Tuyen headed to the door, something stopped her. She felt like she had to stay. To do one more day of work. To prepare one more thing.

And she felt stranger and stranger.

Standing in the single room that she lived in, so uncomfortably spacious now that she was alone, she was afraid. She turned on a light. The bulb worked, but the light seemed dim. And remembering the look of the man, the demon-thing that she had seen in the window of Mystix, she felt a shudder writhe its slow crawl up her spine.

Like Mystix, her apartment was decorated with relics and ornaments from myriad different belief systems. And just as at Mystix, she found little relief looking at any of them.

She wondered how long she had been standing here. How long she had been home. It felt like forever. She couldn't even remember coming home, for that matter. She hoped she had at least remembered to stay at the shop until the day shift guy came to relieve her.

She went to the small refrigerator in the corner of the room and pulled out a pair of items. One was a half-full gallon of milk, which she sniffed and found to be in the "not quite bad" range. Good enough for what she wanted to do. She poured some into a glass with a chipped rim, which was what passed for fine China in this home.

She took the glass of milk and the other item – a brown egg – to the opposite corner of the apartment. There was a small table there, with seven statues on it. They were wooden, each about five inches tall, each worn almost to the point of being featureless, but Gramma had always said they were the strongest things in the apartment.

Tuyen needed strength.

She laid the milk and egg before the statues as an offering and bowed her head to pray. She didn't know what she would say. Didn't know what she could ask for that would help her now.

Something clinked behind her. She turned.

She could see the whole apartment, from the sink and stove and refrigerator in the "kitchen" to the small entertainment console in front of the queen bed. A small bookshelf with works in English and Vietnamese and a second-hand chest of drawers completed the furnishings.

Nothing out of place. Nothing that could have moved. Nothing that could have made a noise.

Yet something had.

A cold wind blew around her, a whirlwind of frigid air, and with it a smell assaulted Tuyen's nose. For a moment she was catapulted back to the final days of Gramma's life, the hours when she had been unable to control her bowels, the life flowing out of her not in poetry and peace, but in a neverending stream of painful diarrhea.

She turned back to the statues.

The milk was there.

The egg was gone. Partly gone.

The white lay in a rancid pool at the feet of the statues, not clear as it should be but yellowed and lumpy. The yolk was gray-green with a brown film. Together they looked like a cancerous eye, staring up at her in mute agony.

It was the source of the smell that pounded at Tuyen, that had started a headache thrumming behind her eyes. The egg was new – she had just bought it a day ago, maybe two – but it had gone rotten in an instant. Curdled by the same force that had made the air chill in her apartment and the blood freeze in her bones.

The shell was gone. There had been no cracking, no

sound of shattering shell. It had just disappeared, leaving a putrified interior behind.

"Bad mojo," she said. She sounded fine. She sounded calm.

But it wasn't true. She wasn't fine, she wasn't calm. Tuyen was terrified. Terrified, and she knew without a doubt that she was in danger of something worse than mere violence. Her offering had been stolen, and mocked. She was being told that she had no help from the old ways. That she could look forward only to corruption.

Tuyen had always been able to see things. But she looked at the corrupt eye of the egg and knew that sometimes sight was a curse; sometimes it was better to be blind.

ANAMNESIS

Evan dropped his keys on a table in the foyer. They jingled and the sound echoed against the tile floor and the echo reminded him how empty the house was.

It had been empty longer than he knew. Longer than he had been prepared to deal with. And even now he wondered if he was really facing it all. If he was ready to admit what had happened, even to himself.

It wasn't easy to find out you had been living with a lie, to find out everything you believed about your life was wrong.

Evan had seen it countless times. In the faces of beaten women who insisted on going back to their husbands because they couldn't quite understand the simple reality that sooner or later their spouses *absolutely* would kill them. In the hostile refusal of young men – boys, really – to testify against leaders in gangs that had left them to rot during robberies that went bad.

Humans excelled at many things – art, war, math. But they were perhaps best at the skill of lying to each other. To themselves.

Would he ever believe – *really* believe – what had happened?

Maybe. Maybe later, when he was a bit farther from everything, when time had given him some perspective, and when he wasn't so bone-weary. He could actually *feel* the circles under his eyes, like red-hot bands that made his eyes burn and his face ache with exhaustion.

A sound interrupted his thoughts. It was low, a gentle squeak. Then another. It sounded like –

(*bedsprings moving, bodies rolling*)

– something moving in the house.

Evan's gun was out before he realized it, full seconds before his mind had drawn the conclusion his body had already reached.

He was alone.

There was no one but him.

But there was a noise. There was a sound.

So something was wrong. Something didn't belong.

He heard the killer, laughing in his mind. The voice saying, "Ring 'round the rosey, then ashes to ashes we all fall down."

He thought about calling Listings. But the idea of calling her about a mere sound, especially *here*, where he had found Val – it was too much. Too hard.

He went in alone.

The living room was first. When Val was alive he had always joked with her that it was the dead room, because no one actually *lived* there at all. It was the room she kept pristine for company, the room that was always clean, always in order.

Not anymore. Evan didn't turn on the lights, but even in the gloom of the pre-dawn morning, he could see the heaps of trash, the coats he hadn't bothered to hang up. It looked lived-in now, if not cared for.

There was nowhere for anyone to hide. And he could see no one.

He moved on.

The kitchen was small and messier than the living room. Takeout boxes, beer bottles. It looked more like the kitchen of a frat house than that of a grown man. Evan supposed that should bother him, but other than his job and Listings, he had found surprisingly little to care about of late.

The sound repeated. A creak.

Evan turned. Back through the living room. Into the hall.

He didn't own a mansion. He was a cop, so he made enough money to subsist at levels that would make a starved alley cat only slightly jealous. The house was small, and the hall had only three doors. All were open: he never had houseguests, so closing up behind him made even less sense than cleaning up last night's kung pao chicken.

But he couldn't see into any of the rooms. And now the sound had stopped.

He led with his gun. Having a firearm was useless if it wasn't at the ready, so he kept it aimed at center-mass-level, ready for anything.

The first room was on the right. A bathroom. The small frosted window in the wall allowed light from the street to stream in, illuminating everything with a ghostly glow.

Nothing in there. There was a bath/shower combo, but the curtain was drawn to the side. Other than that, the only other place anyone could possibly hide was a cabinet under the sink, and Evan decided to take the risk he wasn't being stalked by an undersized midget.

He moved on. The next room. It was a spare bedroom. Someplace that he and Val had talked about furnishing with a crib and toys and some small feet to mess everything up. But after years of trying, they finally realized they weren't going to be able to get the most important of those fixtures.

They talked about turning it into a study. An office. A craft room. A guest bedroom.

It stayed empty and unfurnished.

Evan looked in and saw four walls, an open closet holding only empty space.

And the sound came again.

Squeeeeak.

His heart had been pump-thumping along. Now it began beating at dangerous speeds.

It wasn't his imagination. It was the sound. The *same* sound he had heard before. The day he found Val.

He moved into the hall. Taking footsteps that he knew were normal in size and pace, but that felt like he was pushing through some diabolical combination of cement and Super Glue.

Squeeeeak.

He couldn't see in the last room. The bedroom.

His bedroom, though he slept on the living room couch more often than not.

The door was open, but the angle was bad for him to see in. The darkness seemed to gather around him, to become a cloud that wrapped him not merely in deep blackness, but in a kind of blind terror.

He kept moving forward.

Squeeeeeak. Squeeeeeeeak. Squeeeeeeeeeeeak.

The gun seemed to draw him forward. He wondered if he would have been able to continue without it.

The muzzle pushed into the room. His arm followed. Then his chest. His head.

The darkness fell away from his eyes, the blindness dissipated.

He saw...

... bodies writhing on the bed, under the sheets...

... a beautiful face, looking up at him.

"No!"

Evan fell back a step, his hand going to his face as though he might wash away what he had just seen, what he saw every *moment* of every day. He felt the cold metal of his firearm, smelled gun oil and brass and steel.

He blinked.

The bed was empty. The bodies were gone.

But he wasn't alone.

He didn't know how, but he was certain someone was with him. Behind him.

Warm breath touched his ear. "How long will we dance this dance?" said the killer.

Evan spun, facing the man, almost punching out a shot before realizing that he was alone. The killer was gone. And for a moment Evan wondered if he had ever been there. For a moment he was certain he must have imagined everything that just happened. He was losing it. What had happened to Val had pushed him over the edge.

Then he saw something. It was in the hall, where he had just been standing a moment ago.

He leaned over.

Picked it up.

It was an egg. Not white, but brown, the kind of thing

that farmers and organic food nuts ate. As he picked it up, Evan realized something was wrong with it.

It was light. Insubstantial, almost fake.

He turned it over in his hand, feeling its texture. It had the feel of real eggshell, but even as he felt it, it crumbled in his hands.

There was nothing inside.

Squeeeeeeak.

Evan didn't turn. He didn't look into the bedroom, and he wasn't sure what scared him more: the idea that something was there, or that nothing was.

INTRUSION

Evan called Listings. Then he walked around his house a dozen times, still unsure whether it would be better to find something or not.

He finally sat down on the couch. He had to push aside a blanket and a few coats and something that looked like it might have been a slice of pizza at one point to do it.

He had his gun in his hand the whole time. He wasn't sure what it would do for him against a person who could appear and disappear at will, not to mention the killer's apparent imperviousness to bullets, but it made him feel better to have the thing in his hand.

He sat, but couldn't sit still. He tapped his feet and patted his free hand against his knee.

His gun hand did not move. It remained tight against his right thigh, clamped around the grip of his sidearm, finger on the trigger.

He wondered if he should just get up and do another check of the house, but recognized that if there was anything to be found, he was just going to trample it underfoot by doing that.

So he sat.

And a moment after deciding to remain where he was, Evan fell asleep.

He felt himself sliding into slumber, and part of him was shocked that he could do so. He had just had his home invaded by someone who meant him harm. He was under some kind of attack by forces he didn't understand.

But he was also tired. And his body was screaming at him. He needed rest.

He closed his eyes.

He dreamed.

The dreams were the kind he had been having more and more since Val died: the kind he couldn't remember after waking. He only knew they involved him being in places he didn't want to go. That the people he loved died in the dreams.

That the dreams terrified him.

He felt something tapping on his shoulder. It repeated, and only gradually did he realize that he was feeling something outside of the nightmare that had trapped him. He surfaced slowly, clawing his way out of the fearscape that he had fallen into.

The tap came again.

This time Evan woke. He erupted out of sleep in a blind panic, grabbing for the gun... and realizing it was gone.

No, not gone. It was pointed at him.

Only for a moment, though. Then the muzzled lowered and he could see Listings' face behind it. "And *that* kind of reaction is why I took the pea-shooter away before waking you," she said. Then she pursed her lips and added, "You are a scaredy little man-bitch, aren't you?"

Evan blinked as she put the gun back into his hand, after a moment in which she appeared to be verifying he wasn't going to shoot her with it. He holstered the weapon, still trying to shake off the dream. The unknown dream.

"Thanks for coming," he finally said. He looked around, realizing that daylight was streaming in through the windows, wondering what time it was, wondering how long he had slept.

"Of course." Listings shook her head at the mess in the living room. "See, this is why I never stay over. It has nothing to do with my being a..." and she put up a pair of air-quotes before continuing, "... 'cold-hearted woman who's afraid of her own emotional barriers.' It's –" She broke off, the dry humor leaching out of her voice. "What's wrong? Why'd you call me?"

"He was here."

All traces of humor erased themselves from her face. There was no rage on her face, no fear. Rather it was as though a blank curtain had fallen over her features, covering all emotions and ensuring that no one could get a read on her. But Evan knew her well enough to understand that was her most serious defense mechanism: to withdraw, to hide from the world. She would never run from a physical fight, but she'd hide her feelings. She'd block the world from hurting her heart.

"What?" she said. "The guy? How'd he find your place?"

Evan shrugged. "Same way he found my phone number. And my wife."

"When was he here?"

"Right before I called you. I think."

Listings frowned. "You *think*? What does that mean?"

Evan stood and walked down the hall. He heard Listings follow him. Her footsteps were muffled on the carpet, but they were solid and real. She was one of the last things tethering him to life, one of the last solid anchors he had to a world that had stopped making sense the day Val died.

He stopped at the door to the bedroom. Looking at the bed, part of him here in the hall with Listings, part of him here but on a different day, with a different woman.

"I caught them here," he said. "I don't remember anything of it but her face, looking at me. Like she wasn't surprised. Like she *wanted* me to know."

Listings' voice snapped like a whip. Catching him on the edge of an abyss of self-pity he was about to tumble into. "Focus, White. Where was the bad guy?"

Evan answered, but didn't take his eyes off the empty bed. "He was behind me." He stared at the rumpled sheets, the covers that had rolled into a winding serpent in the middle of the mattress.

Listings looked around the empty hall. "You saw him?" she said.

Evan shook his head. "Just heard him.

Listings put a hand on her head, like this was giving her a headache. "You sure?"

Evan pointed at the small bedside table. "He left a present."

Listings went into the room and looked at the table. "What the hell...?"

She picked up several tiny bits of eggshell from where Evan had placed them after the empty shell shattered in his hand. Then she rubbed her fingers against her jeans, her face crinkling in disgust as she felt the slime that coated the brown and white bits.

Even from here, Evan could smell the greasy layer of scum that covered the shell. Rotten, rank. It smelled like death.

An electronic tone jarred the silence. Listings jerked, then put the bits of shell back on the table and fumbled for her phone.

"Who's the scaredy little man-bitch now?" said Evan.

Listings flipped him the bird. "You only say that because my penis is bigger than yours." Then, before he could offer a rejoinder, she turned on her phone. "Listings," she said. A moment later she nodded, said, "Okay," then turned it off again.

"That was the captain," she said. "Wants us back at the station."

"No rest for the wicked." Evan started to nod, then realized that below the miasma of the egg there was a different smell, something less powerful but still unpleasant. He suddenly realized he was still wearing the same clothes he had walked into the bar with; that he reeked of sweat and fear and the stale odors of a day that had lasted far too long. "Give me a minute to change," he said.

Listings shook her head. "He sounded in a 'now' kind of mood." She looked at the shells. "I'll call the CSI guys and have someone come by and look at this. But we gotta go."

"Captain say what it was about?"

"Yeah, it was that video."

A chill writhed through Evan's spine. He looked at the empty shells on the bedside table. He wondered what they meant.

Listings wiped her fingers on her jeans again. She stared at the bits of egg for a moment, and then walked out.

Evan followed. He didn't want to anger Geist by keeping the captain waiting. He also didn't want to piss

Listings off.

But mostly he didn't want to be alone here in this place that held only the evidence of an impossible intrusion and the memories of the dead.

NOTES

Geist was at the same carrel in the A/V room that Evan had been in. Like Evan, he hadn't changed his clothes – looked like he hadn't gone home at all. That wasn't unusual. The captain was a man who took his job seriously. He was usually at his desk before anyone else arrived on shift, and generally stayed hours after others had closed up shop and left for the day. That was part of why Evan had always trusted the man, had always looked up to him. He was more than a mentor, he was an *example*, in a time and place where examples – at least of the good variety – were harder and harder to come by.

The captain was watching the security tape, staring at the distortions with his face so close to the monitor it looked like he was trying to inhale it. On the desk next to the monitor was a pad, and Geist's hand was going a mile-a-minute as he took notes. Of what, Evan had no idea: whatever the tape held was still a mystery, and anything it held was still locked behind those blurred lines.

"Geist, you read my report yet?" said Listings. The question came as most did from her: without preamble or salutation, as though everyone in the room should already be aware of her, and ready for whatever verbal grenades she might lob their way. Usually she was right in her assumption; she had the kind of presence that people tended to notice.

This time, though, her larger-than-life persona failed her. Geist didn't move his gaze so much as a millimeter. His pen kept racing. All he said was, "Huh?" He sounded dreamy, almost lost. Like he was not just deep in thought, but caught in the throes of some mind-altering experience.

Evan frowned. Geist was a focused person, but this wasn't like him. He would ignore you or tell you to get the hell out of the room and stop bothering him or he would talk to you. This distracted inability to attend to anything other than the television was weird. Not just weird, it was wrong. Geist was acting almost....

Trapped.

"Captain?" said Evan. He caught Listings' eye and saw her face bunched in concern as well.

Geist still didn't look away from the scrambled screen, but he spoke again and sounded a bit more present this time. "You said you got this tape... where?"

"Some cuckoo African voodoo place," said Listings.

"Vietnamese," said Evan automatically.

"Like it matters," said Listings. Then, in a softer tone – one that, as far as Evan knew, his partner reserved only for him and for Geist – she said, "Captain? You find something?"

Geist leaned another fraction of an inch closer to the screen. Any closer and he'd be touching it. "Everything," he murmured. "It's all in here."

Evan looked at Listings again. She shrugged. "Captain," he said, "how long have you been watching this?"

Geist didn't answer. The moment stretched out for a long time, long enough that Evan was about to ask Listings to call the duty officer and ask who was the precinct commanding officer today so they could ask what to do if they had a semi-comatose captain on their hands, when Geist spoke again.

"Over and over," he said. "Just... it's beautiful." He

finally looked away, staring at Evan with the single-minded intensity of a three-year-old struggling to convey something well beyond his vocabulary. "Beautiful," he said again. "The tape loops. It *loops*."

Evan noticed that Geist, now turned almost halfway around to face him, was still writing on his pad. The motion couldn't be comfortable, with his arm almost wrenched behind him. But the older man's hand moved so fast it was a blur, and the *skritch-skritch* of the pen was a subtle scraping at the base of Evan's mind.

"Lots of security tapes do that, Captain," Listings said. Then, in a tone that was even softer: "The tape's messed up, sir. There's nothing there."

Geist swiveled still farther to face Listings.   Still writing.

Skritch-skritch-skritch.

"*Everything's* there," said Geist.   No longer sounding like a child, but now like a zealot.   A fanatic willing to kill or die for what he spoke of.

It started to freak Evan out, and before he even thought about it he was reaching forward to turn off the monitor. He looked at the screen as he did, seeing those strange, twitchy lines, wondering what the captain was seeing in them. Wondering... but at the same time praying he never found out.

"No!"

Geist's shout stopped Evan from moving. The captain stared at him for a second, then as soon as he saw Evan wasn't going to turn off the monitor he turned back and repositioned himself in front of the screen.

Staring at it.

Still writing.

Skritch-skritch-skritch.

"Everything's there," he said. His voice was low, a monotone that sounded like all the emotion had been stripped from it. Evan had investigated a murder a few years ago in which a young couple had been murdered in front of their little boy. When Evan got there, the child – only about five years old, clutching a stuffed animal stained with his parents' blood – had said, over and over, "It's time for bed," in the same voice Geist was using now. The same voice the captain spoke in when he said, "Everything's there. If you watch enough."

Skritch-skritch.

Evan looked at the dancing lines on the screen, and again felt himself drawn in. Felt himself on the verge of seeing something behind the distortion, the truth beneath the chaos. He felt like he was spinning in space, trying to orient on a fixed point in the never-ending twilight of the universe, but with no way to stop himself from turning, turning. Gravity had cut him loose.

"Looks like it's been tampered with," said Listings.

She was right. But as he watched, Evan realized that the captain was also right: there *was* a loop to the images. It was subtle, but the longer he watched the more he saw it. Just a subtle flicker as the screen reset, then played out its encoded secrets, then reset again, then again, and again....

"Ooookay," said Listings, and Evan could tell she was addressing the "You're all acting nuts" tone of her voice to both him and the captain. She reached out and put a hand on the papers that Geist was writing on. "I'm just going to follow up on your research, okay?" she said.

Geist didn't answer. Evan wanted to believe it was because the captain was thinking, was on the verge of some breakthrough that would make everything come to light and restore sense to the world.

But *wanting* to believe wasn't the same as being *able* to.

Listings pulled the papers out from under Geist's hand.

He didn't seem to notice. He kept scribbling, drawing now on the table where the papers had sat. Thick, looping scrawls.

Skritch-skritch-skritch.

Listings handed Evan the papers. He managed to pull himself out of the bent lines of the monitor, out of the looping vision of pandemonium *ad infinitum*. He looked at the papers that Listings had given him.

The sheets were covered in dark scrabbles and scribbles. Nonsense as thick and unremitting as that on the monitor that Geist was still rapturously watching. Every so often there was an actual letter on the papers, but even these seemed so random that they simply added to the disarray rather than implying any sense of underlying meaning. And the fact that all of it was inscribed in the angry scratches of a madman off his meds made it just that much more disconcerting.

Evan looked at Geist. At his friend. "It's all there," said the captain. "It's all there."

Evan couldn't tell if he was talking about the papers or the tape that he was watching so obsessively. And didn't know if it mattered.

"Okay, Captain," said Evan. "We'll... we'll check it out."

Geist nodded, but he was nodding at the monitor, and

Evan couldn't tell if the captain heard him or not. He looked at Listings. She was looking at him with, "What the hell is *this*?" plastered clearly across her features.

Evan didn't know.

MESSAGE

The bodies writhe.

The woman is on the bottom. Evan's wife, *his* wife.

Her name is Val. Not short for Valentine, as so many assume, but rather it is the name of a goddess. She never lets him forget that. She laughs, and the sound is music. "Worship me," she says, and he does.

But now...

He sees them, framed in the open doorway. A body on top, and he cannot see a face. The face is buried in his wife's chest. Buried deep in her bosom, close to her heart. A place Evan thought reserved only for him.

She looks up, perhaps alerted by the scrape of the door opening, the squeak of unoiled hinges. Perhaps it is the muffled sound of his breath, a gasp he cannot hide even as he covers his mouth with his hand.

Maybe it is something else. Maybe she is attuned to this moment. Maybe she has been waiting.

She does not look ashamed. She does not try to stop the man who is moaning against her.

She *smiles*.

She opens her mouth and speaks.

"Hey, White, where are you?"

...

Evan stumbled. The room disappeared, replaced by open air. The carpeting under his feet was gone, and in its place was the cracked and craggy asphalt of the station parking lot.

Listings was looking at him. "Where are you?" she said again, and he suspected that she already knew the answer. Listings knew about Val's cheating, knew about that day.

She had saved Evan from falling into himself, from completely dissolving in pain, especially given what happened after.

But still, it wasn't fair of him to put this on her. She was a good woman – a woman he had no doubt was better than Val had ever been. But that didn't mean he had the right to put the sins of the past on her. To put his baggage on her shoulders, no matter how much she might be willing to bear it.

He tried to bring himself back to the present. Bad enough that they were investigating something tied inextricably to the murder of his wife; he didn't have to mope about finding her in bed with another man while walking with his partner, his –

What do I even call Listings? Girlfriend? Lover? Geez, I suck at this.

He realized he was musing again, lost in thought, and that he still hadn't answered Listings' question. He turned to her.

And his foot caught in another rough patch on the asphalt.

No surprise there, not in a place like Los Angeles, where infrastructure had deteriorated to the point that asphalt was more a theory than a physical reality, where it served more to hold together different potholes and crevices than to actually be a viable surface for smooth walking or driving.

Still, Evan should have been paying better attention. As it was, his arms went up in that automatic reflex we are all born with, the hands pitching forward in a vain attempt to learn to fly at the last second.

He was holding the papers that Geist had been writing on, and when he tripped the loose sheaf of scribbled sheets went flying. They flapped in the air like lame birds, most settling to the ground nearby but a few captured by errant gusts of wind and driven away.

"Dammit!" shouted Listings. She sprinted after the papers, trusting Evan to right himself. Either that or deeming his inevitable fall a suiting punishment for being such a dumb-ass he couldn't manage to walk and talk at the same time.

Hard to tell with her sometimes.

If it was the latter, then she'd be disappointed: Evan managed to stop himself from falling. His fingers skimmed the blacktop and he scraped the pad of his right index finger, but other than that he righted himself without injury.

Listings was already leaning over to grab some of the papers before they spun away. "So the captain is bonkers and my partner's a klutz," she muttered through clearly-clenched teeth.

She wasn't mad. She was afraid.

And then Evan was afraid, too. He grabbed her arm just before she picked up the paper she was reaching for.

He thought for a moment that Listings was going to take a poke at him. She wheeled, her face bleached. People who don't understand what is going on around them most often feel fear, and one of the chief ways humanity has always dealt with fear is through the masking effect of rage. "Hands off, White!"

Evan backed off. He felt the blood rushing out of his face, though for a different reason. His hands went up, trying to placate and calm his partner. "Look," he said, and pointed.

The papers had been scattered when he fell. They had dropped in random piles on the ground, and pressed themselves against curbs, the wheels of a nearby cruiser, a parking meter.

The captain had scrawled letters on the pages. Random letters between the scribbled nothings, letters placed accidentally, letters placed so aimlessly that chaos was their only common descriptor.

Now, when Evan looked at the papers from left to right, the letters on the papers spelled something.

"You see that, right?" he said. His voice was so quiet he didn't know if it made it out of his mouth. Terror clutched his stomach, squeezing everything into his throat.

"What...?" said Listings. For once she had no finish to her sentence.

The letters spelled something.

Not a word.

A message.

I'L KIL Evry 1 U LUv

LOST

Maximillian Geist had tried to be a good captain. A good cop. A good *man*.

When he joined the force it was a different place, a place where you could be a part of the community in ways that were impossible now. The world had been swallowed up by bureaucracies, and how do you do community outreach when you are no longer a hand or a heart, but just a cog? No one understood how to speak to each other, they hid behind walls of legislation and ordinances and rules designed not to protect life, but to protect people from having to *deal* with life.

But Geist kept on. He might be a cog, but he would at least try to be a good cog. His grandfather had been a cop, his father had been a cop. His father had died of complications following a gunshot wound he received when he walked into the middle of a robbery. He wasn't even on duty at the time – just getting some ice cream for Geist's mother during one of her late night "hank'rin's," as she called them.

Hugo Geist entered an all-night convenience store, walked to the dairy section, and made it as far as the cash register with four different kinds of chocolate ice cream before the robber realized he was there and shot him three times in the chest. Geist's father didn't even take a step back. Nor did he drop the ice cream. He simply shifted hands – the store's owner was emphatic about this point to the police and reporters – so that he could hold the ice cream with his other hand, leaving his right hand free to draw the service revolver he always carried with him.

He shot the robber in the throat. The man bled out on

the floor before the store owner could dial 911.

Hugo Geist still didn't fall. He put his gun back. Fumbled out a twenty-dollar bill. Told the owner what it was for.

The ambulance came. They took Hugo away. The next morning his wife got a delivery from the store owner, who brought her the chocolate ice cream in the hospital. He explained that Hugo had wanted to pay for it, and made him promise to take the money needed to pay for it and then use the rest of the twenty as delivery costs to "get Mrs. Geist her ice cream because God knows I'll never hear the end of it if I let a piffly little thing like bullets stop me from getting her her chocolate."

They cried together at Hugo's bedside. He woke up, but was never the same. Infections came and went and he died six months later after losing his right arm, most of his intestinal tract, and all his will to live.

But he was a cop to the end.

That was the way Maximillian grew up: hearing stories of his daddy, the hero. Knowing he would one day be the same kind of man. The same kind of hero.

And he had tried. He had tried... so... *hard.*

But the bureaucracies. And the rules. And the gangs. And the million other things.

And there was the one thing. That *one* thing. The one thing that Geist knew would always haunt him, would always stand between him and the dream he had of being not only a hero, but a genuinely *good man.*

Maybe that was why he was so fascinated by this tape. Maybe that was why he was watching it, staring at it as the lines spun and whirled in front of him. He felt like it was dragging the memories out of him. Pulling him away from the pain, from the mistakes.

It was also pulling him away from the good. From the joy. From all that made him who he was, and who he might one day become.

He wondered if it was killing him.

But even that thought seemed to be plucked from his mind by the strange, almost pulsating vision on the screen in front of him.

I am empty.

I have made no mistake.

Not even the one mistake.

Not even the one.

Geist leaned in closer to the television screen. He was so close that he could feel the static of the screen pulling at the small hairs of his face – his eyebrows, the bit of stubble he'd accumulated. So close that the screen fogged a bit with each breath.

Almost close enough to rest against.

What happens if I touch the screen?

He didn't do it.

Not yet.

Something clicked, and he realized that the lights in the already-dim A/V room had gone out. He couldn't tell if someone else was in the room with him. He didn't think so.

He knew he should be concerned about that. The lights going out, but no one touching them? And it couldn't be a fuse blowing, because the TV was still on.

The tape was still playing.

The tape.

The... tape....

Geist leaned just a fraction of an inch closer.

The thoughts poured out of his mind.

PARTNERS

Angela Listings was a woman with secrets.

The thing about secrets, though, was that they invited discovery. No one ever bothered to read a mystery about a person who told everything to everyone. So sometimes Listings wondered if it might be better to simply share everything about her past with someone.

Evan knew a lot of it. Knew almost all of it, in fact.

But even he didn't know everything. Even he didn't know all her mysteries.

Still, he knew a lot. And that was probably the only reason she was still here, stepping through a doorway that looked like someone had decorated it in Early Rainforest. She didn't much care about the guy they were following – not the way he did, that was for sure.

And that was odd for her. Because caring about the bad guy had been her guiding light, her central characteristic, for nearly all her life.

When she was seven years old, Listings saw her first dead man. That dead man was the reason she hated criminals, but not the reason she was a cop. The *second* dead man was why she was a cop.

The second dead man came into her house when she was asleep. Not dead yet, but so wired on speed that it had to be only a matter of time before his heart burst in his chest. Her father tried to stop him, but the drugs in the man's body let him shrug off her father's punches and kicks like they were nothing more than the flitting wings of a hummingbird.

The addict wasn't looking for anything. He wasn't there for money, he wasn't seeking sanctuary from police.

He just wanted to destroy something. First himself. Then the door to their house. Then Listings' father.

The junkie broke her dad in pieces, right in front of her. She had pulled herself out of bed in time to see the man grimly twist her dad's arm right out of its socket.

Listings never knew her mother, who had fled family life soon after her birth in search of "her center" – whatever the hell that meant. So her father was her hero. Her protector, her savior. He was her *world*.

She had never heard him scream like that, the way he did when the crazed addict pulled out his arm. But the sound of her daddy's scream weren't nearly as bad as the scraping shriek of the junkie's laugh as he did it.

The man was tall and wiry. He wore no shirt, and his torso was covered in scrapes. Some were self-inflicted, but it would later be discovered that this was his fourth visit to a home. That her father was the fifth man the junkie had killed.

Little Listings – only she was Angela then, and Angie to her daddy – came down the hall in time to slip on a gout of blood. She didn't scream. She was too shocked to scream, too scared at the sight of the superhero she had worshiped all her life being torn apart like a fly at the hands of a schoolyard bully.

She didn't scream.

The junkie saw her anyway. Probably heard her foot slapping down in the blood, or the intake of her breath as she choked back a sob.

He looked at her, and she saw that he had scratched his

cheeks. One of his eyelids seemed to hang askew.

He grinned through bloody teeth. Then made a sound like a dog dismissing an unsavory treat, and turned back to her father. He started *tickling* her daddy. Still laughing.

Her daddy didn't laugh at the tickles. He didn't scream anymore, either. His eyes were staring at nothing, his cheeks covered in his own blood like the makeup of a strange clown.

Listings saw her first dead man. The one who gave her an eternal hatred of those who would unjustly harm others, who would steal the life and livelihood from those weaker than them.

She saw her second dead man a moment later. She still didn't scream. She *did* cry. Cried so much the tears cast a shimmering veil over her sight and made it that much harder for her to do what she had to. That much harder to get the gun out of her father's bedside table. That much harder to load it with the bullets he kept in a separate drawer. That much harder to chamber a round. That much harder to walk back down the hall to where the addict was still tickling her father's corpse.

Then she walked in her father's blood, and the tears disappeared and suddenly it was not hard at all.

She put the gun against the junkie's head, right over the shredded eyelid, and pulled the trigger.

And knew she would have to be a police officer. Not because she had a desire to right wrongs, though there was a bit of that. No, she had to grow up to be a police officer because in the instant she blew away the man who killed her daddy she felt *delicious*. She felt *right*.

She would kill the bad guys. That was what she would

do.

Daddy would never come back. Her superhero was gone.

So she would have to be the superhero.

But even at seven, Angie knew that superheroes didn't exist – at least not the way they were shown in movies. She would have to grow up to be something that would let her beat up and kill the men like the one who killed her father.

She would kill them all.

It was hard. Hard becoming a cop. Hard reigning herself in sometimes, when she just wanted to let fly and give in to the urge to turn someone's face into hamburger.

Hardest of all had been partnering up with people who she knew would never understand, would never forgive her for what she wanted to do.

Evan had been the first one to break her self-imposed isolation. He had pried back the walls of her obstinacy, had hammered down the barricades of anger and silence that she had so carefully erected over the years.

She told him everything.

And he didn't judge her. He said, "I hope you don't kill anyone with me." But that was it. He didn't ask if she *had* killed anyone – she hadn't – or if she would do it in the future. Just asked her not to do it around him. Like he knew he couldn't change her, but thought she was worthy of her job, worthy of the work she was doing.

Worthy of him?

She glanced at him as he followed her into the weird shop. Mystix, it was called, and she thought that was an odd choice. It sounded like a New Age smokehouse, but inside it looked like someone had barfed the religious equivalent of alphabet soup all over the place.

"Tell me why we're here again?" she said. She was hoping he'd make a joke, would at least smile. He'd been quiet since his wife was murdered, and that was certainly understandable. But after they kissed that first time, after they held each other and then went to her place and held each other through the night, he had seemed happy. At peace.

She felt good. Not like she did when she busted a pervert or got the chance to pummel some douchebag. No, she felt like maybe she wasn't just patching holes in the underpinnings of a crumbling society. She was actually *building* something. She wasn't repairing, she was creating. Making something out of nothing but the feelings that existed between them. Out of nothing but his beautiful smile.

But his smile was fading again, and more so since that call had come, since she had met him at the bar. Just a night ago, and he was falling back into the malaise that had gripped him after Val's death.

"We're looking for the little Vietnamese girl I saw in the alley," said Evan.

"This place is freakin' creepy," she said, letting him step forward to take the lead.

"You should see it at night," he said.

There were a pair of old women browsing the shelves, picking up bits of herby-looking plants, sniffing them condescendingly, replacing them, then grabbing the next bundle of greenery for olfactory review. Both looked like they were probably about six hundred years old, stubby bodies and round faces that made Listings feel like she was probably looking at the original body doubles for Buddha.

Evan had already spotted the old broads and was moving toward what Listings guessed passed for the checkout counter: a rickety stool with a cash register sitting on it. Behind the stool was a guy who was just as stubby as the old ladies, only he looked like he weighed twice as much as the two of them combined. Maybe five feet tall, and just as wide. The fact that he was wearing a neon pink shirt that looked like it had exploded through a vibrant wormhole that led direct to the worst parts of eighties fashion served only to exaggerate his bulk.

He was reading a Bible. And seemed intent on continuing his reading regardless of the presence of potential new customers in the store. Most Asians that Listings ran into were polite and helpful – more courteous than the average white person, that was for sure. But there were exceptions. People stuck in the "old world," where concepts of racial superiority still held sway. Bigots were bigots, whatever color or stripe.

Listings suspected this guy might be one of those types who wouldn't deign to speak to anyone with the wrong pedigree. He didn't even twitch when Evan walked up to the register and laid a hand on it. The stool creaked, and still the guy didn't deign to acknowledge them.

Dozens of necklaces encircled the man's thick neck. Religious totems. Silver crucifixes, a gold Star of David, what looked like a jade Buddhist Lotus knot, and a few others that she couldn't identify. They tangled into one another, a strangely beautiful chaos. The Lotus knot in particular was a gorgeous piece, turning into itself, twisting into infinity.

"Excuse me," said Evan. "Is the girl from last night available?"

The chubby dude kept on doing his thing.

Evan sighed. He dug his wallet out of his jacket pocket and flipped it open. The badge caught the gleam of one of the overhead lights and reflected against Fatty's eyes. Fatty did not seem impressed. Listings would have said he was the definition of "inscrutable," but she thought that would probably get her a department write-up for inappropriate racial stereotyping. Even if it fit in this situation.

"It's important," said Evan, irritation creeping into the cracks that exhaustion and stress was opening in his voice. "Police business."

He looked like he might have said something else, but Listings was done. The dude behind the register might be a bad guy, or he might not. But he was *definitely* being an asshole, and that qualified him for the Fear-Of-God treatment, at the very least.

"Hey, Tubby," she said. "Do you want to help me and my partner in crime here, or do you want to spend the day with your shop closed? Huh?" She clapped her hands together. "Shop-o shut-o?"

Evan pinched his nose between thumb and forefinger. "He's Vietnamese. I don't think imitation Spanish will help."

Tubby sighed and closed his Bible.

Listings grinned at Evan. Then felt her grin crack into several pieces and fall away like porcelain left too long in a kiln as Tubby started speaking. Low, even tones, words burbling by so fast that Listings doubted she could have followed them even if she *did* speak Vietnamese. Which she definitely did not.

The guy kept talking, and she wondered if she should flash her *own* badge. There was a legitimate chance the guy didn't speak English, but if he had intended to cooperate he would have made some motion of doing so already, so....

The old ladies who had been shopping for Vietnamese paprika or whatever it was stepped toward the side of the register. Tubby didn't stop talking, just took their money and made change and never stopped his monotone rant.

Evan looked at Listings with a dry smile. "Do you want to write this down, or should I?"

She loved him for making the joke. She also kind of wanted to punch his teeth down his neck.

Evan turned back to Tubby, who still hadn't stopped. "We're gonna go in the back, okay?"

Tubby continued his screed. Evan shrugged. He looked at Listings. "Think that's a yes?" he said.

"Sounds like one to me."

Evan led the way to the back of the shop. Tubby never stopped talking, not even as they stepped through a thick black curtain at the rear of the store.

The front of the store had been religious alphabet soup. All iconography and crystals and the stuff that hopes are made of. The back of the store was different. It was where hopes came, not to die, but to be tortured at the hands of angry demons. The kinds of monsters who knew that sometimes death was a release, a relief, and so would never let the torture end, would never let the suffering abate.

Hope would wither here. It would shrivel. It would twist and contort and become something ugly and terrible.

But it wouldn't die.

"Cheery," she said. Sarcasm, always her first defense, the armor she had worn at almost every moment since her father's death. "What's this, the voodoo aisle?"

Evan shook his head as he walked slowly into the dark area. "Hmong," he said.

"What's that?"

"Beat's me." He threw a half-smile over his shoulder. "I'd guess it's Vietnamese for 'the voodoo aisle.'" He turned forward again, but continued. "I liked the 'partners in crime' thing, by the way. That how you see us?"

Listings shrugged. A wasted gesture since Evan wasn't looking at her, but she felt like she had to make everything an exaggeration here. Like she had to remind the world – and herself – that she was still alive. That the sonofabitch who pulled her father apart hadn't gotten her as well; that she was still kicking ass and taking names. "Well, it had that special something," she said. Then: "Why are we here?"

Evan pointed at an open door just ahead. It was dark inside. The doorway looked like the entrance to a cellar, though such were rare in Los Angeles.

Evan passed through the portal and disappeared.

She wondered if she would disappear if she followed him.

But she knew she would follow him regardless. Because he needed her. Because she needed him.

And because they *were* partners in crime, after all.

GUIDED

Evan stepped into the back office, moving into the place with the surety and security of a man stepping into his own home. He had only been there once with Tuyen, but he wasn't worried about hitting anything in the dark. Part of that was simply because there was nothing to hit.

Mostly, though, was the sense that had gripped him. The feeling that he was being guided. Led. Like he had been stripped of his ability to choose what his next steps would be. And he didn't even mind: the lack of agency was not confining, but liberating. As though his entire life had been a prison, and now in the moment of surrendering to an inexorable fate he had finally found peace.

He turned on the light. His hand found the switch easily, flicking it on as he moved into the windowless room.

The security monitor was still in its cabinet above the computer. It was off, dimly reflecting the contents of the room. He turned it on. It came to life with a low hum, static illuminating its surface.

Evan flipped on the computer's power switch.

"We might want to get *actual* permission before digging through this guy's stuff," said Listings. She sounded oddly restrained.

"We might," he said. He waited a moment for the computer to power up, but it did nothing. Dead. Whether it had always been like this, or whether it had recently been sabotaged to preclude anyone looking into its files he could not say.

"Is it even plugged in?" he said. He was speaking mostly to himself, but Listings responded.

"Can't tell. What are we looking for?"

"The address of the girl I talked to. Or her phone number. Something."

The desk on which the computer sat had a pair of drawers. Neither was locked. He opened the top one and pulled out a few papers at random.

Everything was written in Vietnamese. Or what he assumed was Vietnamese – it could have been ancient Sanskrit for all he knew. "And I took Spanish in high school," he said.

Evan heard a metallic click as Listings opened the file cabinet that was jammed into the back of the tiny room. "What a waste, right?" she said. "I managed to avoid taking a foreign language, myself."

"How'd you manage that?"

"Threats."

Evan snorted. Though he wasn't entirely sure she was joking. Before he could ask, Listings added, "What's the girl's name? The one we're looking for?"

"Tuyen," he said.

"Is that a first or a last name?"

"That's what I said." Listings looked at Evan blankly, so he clarified. "She wasn't super-chatty."

Listings nodded, then returned to the file cabinet. Evan kept peeling through the papers in the computer desk. All of them were incomprehensible. The few that were in English were generic bills. Nothing helpful.

Listings made a sound. Evan turned to see her pulling

something out of the back of the top drawer of the file cabinet. "Huh," she said.

"Something?"

"Looks like."

She handed Evan a sheet of paper. He recognized it immediately. He had never seen this particular one, but had definitely seen others like it. It was a "New Hire" sheet, the kind of things businesses put together for employees, with spots for home addresses, home and cell phone numbers, emails, and so on.

This one was mostly blank. A few Vietnamese characters.

And the name "Tuyen" across the top in bold letters, along with a phone number and an address.

"Great!" said Evan. He felt strange holding the paper. One step closer to understanding what had happened in the last few hours to turn his life into such a strange place, perhaps, but shouldn't that make him feel *better*? Instead he felt weird, felt like running straight to the address on the paper, or phoning the number and –

He weaved on his feet. His knees wobbled under his frame, the odd sensation that he was both here with Listings and at the same time absent from his body taking hold of him. He staggered.

"What?" said Listings. "What is it?"

Evan looked closer at the paper. Confirmed what he had seen. What he *thought* he had seen.

And it was there. It was true.

He pointed at the paper. At the bottom of the paper someone had written "Alt. Phone," followed by a number.

Listings was shaking her head, clearly not understanding.

Evan knew how she felt. He didn't understand, either. He tapped the number. "That's Val's cell number," he said.

Listings' gaze shot from the page in Evan's hand to his eyes. "Your wife's number?" she said. She frowned, looking at the sheet. "Why would some Vietnamese voodoo rave chick have that number listed as her second phone?"

Evan couldn't answer. He shook his head. Stunned. He turned away from Listings for a moment, turning back toward the computer desk. He needed to look away from her. She was his partner, his friend, his... whatever they were.

But he needed to look away. Needed not to be distracted by her presence and the feelings he was having for her.

He looked at the paper.

Why is Val's number on this?

Why did the killer call me?

Why didn't he die *when I shot him?*

Something moved in Evan's peripheral vision. He looked up at the security monitor. It had shifted, the static gone. In its place....

Bodies writhing. A woman on the bottom. Evan's wife. Looking at the camera, looking at *him*. Val smiled. Opened her mouth to speak, but before he could –

"No!"

Evan swept the monitor off the shelf. It crashed to the floor with an electric snap, followed by the sharp crack of shearing glass. Tiny bits of the screen smashed across the floor in a white wave, like a strangely sharp invasion of insects.

"What the hell?" Listings half-shouted.

"Didn't you... didn't you see?" Evan could barely put three words together.

Sounds came from the front of the shop, beyond the curtain.

"Time to go," said Listings. She grabbed his arm and began pulling him out of the office.

Evan stared at the floor. Then he saw the computer – the lifeless, useless computer – turn on. The computer screen lit up with the same thing he had seen on the security monitor: the scene from his bedroom. Val, smiling at him. A nameless, faceless man burrowing into her.

She smiled at him, smiled from beyond the grave, smiled from beyond death itself. Still beautiful, so beautiful that the mere sight of her – even like this – had a power he didn't know how to combat.

Listings dragged him away.

She didn't see it.

She didn't see.

That sense of being led, of being taken in hand and guided through a predestined series of steps, was still very much present. But the peace it had imparted was gone. Evan was being guided someplace, and he didn't know if it was a place of darkness or light.

The dark arts in the back of the shop seemed much darker. The trio of creatures consuming one another – snake, monkey, jackal – stared with accusing eyes at him.

Were their eyes open before? Weren't they closed?

The world slipped out from under him. The creatures each had one white eye, one black one. A dichotomy of darkness and light that some might interpret as harmony or balance, but that Evan sensed meant something more ominous.

Were *their eyes open before?*

The curtain parted. The fat proprietor passed into the back of the store. He was still holding his Bible, still letting loose with a non-stop torrent of Vietnamese, delivered in an intense monotone. It sounded like he hadn't stopped since responding to Listings however many minutes –

(*hours? days? years?*)

– ago. But then he stopped abruptly as he spotted the broken closed circuit monitor, the pieces all over the floor.

Listings dragged Evan past him. Right through the curtain. The fat man started screaming shrilly. Still in Vietnamese, but there was no mistaking the anger in his voice.

"We'll call you with a billing address for that," shouted Listings.

Then she dragged Evan past the shelves at the front of the shop, through the bamboo door-hanging. Outside.

But his confusion and fear came with him. He thought they might have come to stay.

QUESTION

Listings listened to the tinny voice in her ear repeat the message one more time, then ended the call.

"It says the number is no longer in service," she said. She looked at the paper they had taken from the Mystix office, the one that had this Tuyen girl's phone number, along with the second, the "Alt. Phone" at the bottom. "You sure the other one belonged to your wife?"

She immediately knew that was the wrong thing to say. Evan had been acting extra-wiggy since... whatever it was had caused him to flip in the back of the store. His face was sheet white except for two bright fever spots, one on each cheek. He looked like he'd not only seen a ghost, but perhaps been possessed by one.

He laughed at her question, a laugh so utterly bereft of mirth that it stole the warmth from her body as quickly as any winter wind could have. "Pretty sure. I used to call it ten times a day. Before I found out she was banging her way through our marriage."

Listings' mouth pulled itself into a firm line. She felt the part of herself that had blown away the junkie surfacing, the part of herself that was in charge of the thin line where justice and vengeance intersected. And she knew they *did* intersect. Some crimes were so evil, so heinous, that only by allowing the victims the opportunity to levy the execution could any justice be found.

"I would've killed her," she said. And again knew that it was the wrong thing to say. Not because Evan looked any worse for the statement – the only way he could possibly look worse would be to drop dead right in front of her – but because it just wasn't morally cool to say something like that to a man whose wife had been murdered the way Evan's had.

Even if the death had allowed Listings her first chance at happiness, at *real* happiness, since her father died.

But Evan didn't seem to mind. That chilling laugh came again. "Well it looks like our guy beat me to it," he said. Listings hated hearing that. He was closing down, and that wasn't what she loved in him. He'd always been an open book, had always been the one who could share anything.

Don't shut me out, Evan. I'm here for you. I'll understand, I'll believe.

But she didn't say that. That wouldn't have been her.

Evan closed his eyes. They were standing only a few steps away from the entrance to Mystix, and Listings fully expected Tubby the Religious to come waddling after them at any moment. But he hadn't. They were alone, and that was good because Evan looked like he was about to drop.

"Maybe I should let this go," he said.

"I told you, Romeo," she said. "I need your protection like you need a stiff kick in the balls."

"No." He shook his head. "Not for that. It's just...." He took the paper from her hand. Stared at it for a long time, his eyes traveling from the phone number listed at the top – the primary number that was now "no longer in service" – to the one listed at the bottom. His wife's cell number.

"I've gone over it a million times, Listings," he whispered. "I get a message telling me she called and needed me to come home. And when I get there...." His eyes were blank, almost non-reflective as he fell into the memory.

Listings understood what that was like; knew better than to try to pull him out of it.

"There she was. I fell over, Listings. I goddam fell *over* I was so surprised. And when I got up the guy was gone. Ran through the back door like a thief." He gulped and looked at the ground. At the sky. Anywhere but at her. "I left like a thief, too. Then she's dead a few hours later. And you know what the last thing she said to me was?"

He looked at her now. His eyes boring into her soul. She could see pain in his eyes, but wondered if she was seeing his pain, or merely her own reflected in his gaze. "The last words I heard from my wife's lips were, 'You had to find out sooner or later. Close the door on the way out.'"

"Bitch." Listings spat the word. Not just a description, not just an empty term of vituperation, but a true curse. She had resented Val for a long time, because she had sensed what Evan seemed determined not to see. But when she saw what the woman had done to Evan, what she had turned him into, the resentment refined itself to rage.

Evan passed a hand over his eyes, as though trying to wipe away the memories that must assail him. "I loved her, Listings," he said.

The words twisted in her heart. Not like a knife, nothing so merciful. More like a fist wrapped in barbed-wire, gouging its way painfully to her most secret parts, to the hidden Listings, the Angie that no one saw. She knew that Evan had loved his wife. It was the nature of good people to love others, even when the ones they loved were unworthy of that affection. And Evan had been good. So good.

But she hoped that when Val died, he could have turned away from her. Could have turned away from the

114

cold corpse of an unfaithful wife, and held tight to Listings instead. And she would never hurt him, because she was his partner, and partners looked out for each other. She would protect him, and he would protect her.

"Do you still?" she said. "Do you still love Val?"

She didn't want to know. But she had to find out. Because the one thing she couldn't do anymore was share Evan, especially not with a dead woman.

Evan didn't answer. They stood alone in the shadow of a nothing shop in a crap part of the city for far too long. Acting out what felt to Listings like a ridiculous scene in the kind of movie she avoided, but the kind of movie that could be seen playing over and over in theaters through the world.

She wouldn't share him. She wouldn't. She had done so much for him, had busted her ass for him. She deserved better than half a heart.

So how was it that she found herself reaching for him? About to touch his shoulder, maybe even pull him in for a hug right there in public.

Evan was still staring at his feet, looking down like the secrets of the universe might be discovered in the cracked cement of the sidewalk.

She pulled her hand back when he abruptly moved. She didn't know if he saw her reaching for him. Didn't know if he was rebuffing her attempt to reach out – not just to reach out to him, but to reach out beyond her own self, her own limits. Maybe he hadn't seen her at all. Maybe he was simply trying to avoid the question she had asked about Val. Maybe he didn't even know an answer.

No matter what, he didn't look at her. He just swung about and headed down the street. "Come on," he said.

Listings wanted to turn away. To go the opposite direction and never talk to him again. But she didn't. She followed him.

As she knew she would.

As she *had* to do.

EVIDENCE

Working as a cop, Evan had spent time in a lot of disturbing places. Crack houses, murder scenes, even Mystix were all sufficient to give him a case of the willies.

Still, though he recognized a surplus of disturbing places in the world, he also knew that a few were not merely disturbing, but actually disturbed. Places that had seen so much evil that such had become a part of what held them together, as much a part of the structure as brick or mortar.

The evidence locker was one of those places.

It wasn't really a locker, it was an entire room that took up half the basement. But it had the feel of a huge locker, something utilitarian and overused and grimy. A cage and a gate sat at the front to keep out the uninitiated. Beyond it, though, a person could freely walk among shelf after shelf, sheets of metal piled high. And on each cold piece of metal lay boxes, neatly labeled and sealed. Some were cardboard, some plastic. Each box cradled the wrecked remains of a life, pitiful testaments of death come too soon.

Labels adorned the boxes, listing contents in neat columns as though order outside might hold back the chaos straining within. Evan tried not to look at them when he came in here. He tried to look only at what he absolutely needed to see. As if to look at more than what was necessary would lead inevitably to more boxes, more labels.

A lot of cops were superstitious. They had their rituals designed to keep them safe: left sock on first, crucifix under the vest but over the undershirt, never take a dump in the first hour of your shift. The customs and rites would look ridiculous to an outsider, but to the police on whose lives the smallest details could mean the difference between life and death, and for whom so much was a matter of blind, random chance, such silly details were a moment of control. A last chance to assert themselves over the impartiality of fate.

Evan had never participated in those rituals. Had never allowed himself to believe that by tying his shoes right over left instead of left over right he could somehow forestall death when it came for him. But he could not look at the boxes more than was necessary. Could not stay longer than he had to in this place where every word was a catalogue of violence and evil and death.

Still, no matter how hard he tried he always saw. Sometimes you were blind when you tried to see, sometimes you tried to close your eyes and discovered your vision went on forever.

He walked down the center aisle that bisected the evidence room, Listings close behind. She looked at everything, head swiveling left and right like she was in a museum.

And even though Evan didn't want to look, he couldn't help but see.

A gun in a plastic bag....

A kilo of dope, wrapped in duct tape that had been torn by angry teeth....

A translucent box that held a single bottle with what looked like a severed hand floating in formaldehyde....

Evan looked at his feet. He didn't want to see. Even though he was going to the worst place in the room, the one place that was more terrible than all the others combined.

The echoes of his and Listings' footsteps bounced around them, resounding into eternity. It sounded like they were in a crowd, but a crowd of invisible people who left only traces of themselves behind.

A uniformed cop appeared from one of the side aisles. Evan didn't know him, and didn't want to risk chatting with someone he didn't know. He turned aside before the cop saw him, and he and Listings busied themselves with the contents list of a box halfway down a different aisle.

The cop shuffled papers. He sounded like he was logging new evidence. A moment later he appeared in the center aisle and walked past them. The gate clanked and clicked as he opened then closed it behind him. A few muffled words with the duty officer at the gate. They both laughed.

Then silence.

Evan and Listings moved back into the center of the room.

"I hate this place," said Listings.

"Yeah, it could use a paint job." The joke fell flat, delivered in a grim monotone.

Listings didn't notice. "It's not that. Just... it goes on forever. All of these little boxes are bits of people's hate, reminders of humanity's inhumanity. And it seems like you could walk around in here for a lifetime and keep on being surprised at how low it goes." She touched a box. One of the clear plastic bins, sheaves of papers and what looked like blood-spattered clothes inside. "All these crimes, repeated over and over, each one different. But at the same time so much the same."

Evan couldn't help but smile a bit. He knew her past.

Knew what she had done, what she had had to do. That she had survived made her someone to be respected. That she had avoided turning into a monster... it was the foundation of what he loved about her. Her resistance to evil. Her commitment to save other victims.

"I didn't know you were such a poet," he said.

She smiled back at him, that cynical smile of hers. "I'm amazing in the sack, too."

"I knew that." Her smile turned genuine, and he liked it enough she was in danger of being kissed right then. He didn't want to get derailed, so he added, "That many men's room limericks can't be wrong. 'There was a cop named Listings with great luck, who really liked –"

He shut up long enough to duck the punch she sent at his nose. She was smiling, she still looked lovely, but he couldn't kiss her *and* bob and weave, so his concentration was back.

Besides....

"Here we are."

He turned down an aisle at the back of the room. It was darker here, as though even the light shunned this part of the room.

Evan went immediately to the boxes he had come for. He had only seen them once, but they were burned on his mind. Each bore an identical case number, the names of the lead investigators on the case. Geist's name was on the boxes. So was Listings'.

Evan's was not. At least, not as an investigator.

He opened several of the boxes. They were cardboard bankers boxes with flip tops that came off easily, exposing the contents.

"You know you're screwing up the custody chain," said Listings in a low voice. "When we find the guy who did it, it's gonna be that much harder to keep him if anyone finds out about this. Even a court-appointed lawyer with a head injury and a drinking problem could get him off."

Evan ignored her. She was right, of course: part of any major case involved proving that the evidence was in pristine shape, that it hadn't been tampered with in any way. That involved proving it was always in the control of someone responsible, that access to it was limited and logged, that no one ever had a chance to alter or manipulate it. Without proving chain of custody, important evidence became fodder for objections, often inadmissible.

But Evan had to find out what was going on. He had to know.

And no one was investigating this case anymore.

The first box didn't have anything useful. He opened another box. Inside: a mass of sheets. Tagged and bagged in clear plastic. The sheets were light blue. They had been a gift from Val.

They were bloody.

He touched them, and touching them remembered. Not just the entrance, not just the shock of seeing his wife and the man. Not just her smile and the matter-of-fact way she spoke to him.

No, now he remembered her as she was when he came back later in the day: laying on the bed, covered in the same sheets that had tangled her and her lover. Still smiling that same cold smile, only now she smiled not at him but at the ceiling. And she wore an extra smile as well, a thin red smile that stretched from one ear to another, blood no longer pumping from her throat but already starting to congeal.

A knife stood up, skewering her breast so deeply that Listings later told Evan it had punched all the way to the hilt, had nearly severed Val's spine.

Evan closed the box with the sheets. He hoped he found what he was looking for before he opened the box with the knife. He didn't want to see that.

He opened another box.

Another.

Listings was looking over his shoulder. He could sense tension coming off her. He didn't know if it was that they were breaking regs by doing this, that she was worried about him, or just the situation in general.

"I never saw a case move to the cold files so fast," she said.

Evan shrugged. He pasted as neutral a look on his face as he could. Emotions swirled hard and fast, and he didn't trust himself to show any of them right now.

"No prints, no evidence to speak of. No nothing." He let loose a single breath, what passed for a laugh. "Not that they told me much."

Listings looked genuinely remorseful. "Geist and I tried. We tried our best to keep things moving the way you'd want –"

Evan waved her to silence. "Even a cop's wife can't keep the department busy for too long." He laughed again, this time a bit more under control. "We can't buy working computers, we're hardly going to spend forever on a dead-end case."

He sighed. Inhaled. Tore into another box.

"What are we looking for?"

There were two more boxes. One would hold the knife.

He opened the closest box. Exhaled sharply. Relief sagged his features for a moment.

He reached inside and drew out a book. "This," he said.

It was a planner. The kind of thing used by the classy, the pretentious, people who hated computers, and folks who were combinations of the three. He had always assumed Val belonged to the first group. Now he knew differently.

"Her Day-Timer?" Listings' brow furrowed as Evan unclasped the leather cover and began flipping through the pages. He turned to the section that held phone numbers and addresses. "The investigating detectives would've looked through that already."

"Yup," said Evan.

"So what are *you* doing?"

"Same thing." His eyes scanned each page quickly. Nothing... nothing... nothing... noth –

He smiled. "But I know a few things they don't," he said. He held up the planner, showing one of the pages to Listings.

"What am I looking at?" she said.

He tapped a number at the bottom of the page. There was no name above it. "This is the only number that I don't recognize in my wife's book. You wanna guess whose number it is?"

"The guy she was doinking?"

"Hardly.   She wouldn't have left that out in plain sight."

You sure about that?

That cold smile.

"You had to find out sooner or later.   Close the door when you leave."

"Then who?"

Evan forced himself back to the present.   He couldn't afford to slip, couldn't afford to lose control of himself.

"Ten to one it's Tuyen's number."

"It was disconnected."

He shook his head.   "The one on her new hire form was.   But this is," he said, tapping the planner again, "is more recent.   And it's different from the one on the form.   I bet it's her current number."

Listings thought about it.   Evan could see the wheels turning, could see her looking for a reason that couldn't be right.   It was just a hunch, but it was a good one.   Tuyen had listed Val's number as her secondary contact.   Val had some kind of connection to the girl.

Who *was* Tuyen?

What did she have to do with Val, and with the man Evan had shot; the man who should be *dead*… but wasn't?

The man who should be dead….

That thought sent shudders up and down Evan's spine. Not just because he didn't understand what was going on, but because some deep part of him *did* understand… and was so terrified at the truth that it had hidden deep in the blackest recesses of his own mind.

Listings nodded. "Wow."

"Yeah. Wow." He pulled out his cell and began to dial the number on the page.

"Won't work down here," said Listings. She gestured around them. "Too much steel and concrete to get a signal."

Evan rolled his eyes. "Nothing's ever easy."

"Not if you wanna keep breathing."

He started to pocket the planner. "Come on."

Listings put a hand on his, stopping his motion. "Chain of custody, White." She motioned at the planner. "It's gotta stay here."

Evan tore loose. "*Screw* chain of custody. I want to find this bastard."

Listings looked like she was going to either argue with him or shoot him. Evan wasn't sure which would be worse. But he wouldn't back down either way. He couldn't afford to. Muddling up the chain of custody wouldn't cost him anything at this point, and –

And a noise stopped the argument/shooting before it began.

It was a solid thud. Nothing that Evan could identify, but it sounded wrong. Something that didn't belong here. Something alien and dangerous.

Listings looked at him and he could see she was thinking the same thing. She raised her eyebrows, a "What was that?" movement he'd seen a thousand times.

He shrugged. He felt like pulling his sidearm, but that would have been ridiculous.

The lights started flickering slowly. Less like a loose wire than like a pulse, pounding faster and faster.

Listings peeked around the corner of the shelves, like she was worried about an attack, then slid into the center aisle

The lights flickered faster. Then the flickers became arrhythmic: no longer a panicked pulse but the stammering beats of someone in the middle of a cardiac arrest.

Evan passed Listings. Leading her into the center aisle. Both of them were on their guard, neither sure why.

The lights went out.

He heard Listings draw her gun; he did the same. Both of them took cover automatically. Listings darted left and he moved right, each of them tucking in behind one of the huge shelving units on either side of the center aisle.

The darkness wasn't complete, but nearly so. The ceiling had been swallowed, and the shelves had become boxy skeletons, looming in this museum of mayhem and cloaked not in flesh and bone but in the proofs of violence.

"White?" whispered Listings.

"Where's the duty officer?" he said. The officer at the front of the evidence area should have been back here, checking to make sure nothing was wrong. Preserving evidentiary integrity, making sure the chain of custody stayed intact.

"I don't know, but he's getting his ass kicked."

BAM.

The sound of something heavy slamming into metal. Then a pause that seemed terribly long, but couldn't have been more than a second or two.

WHAM.

CRASH.

Evan looked at Listings, barely able to make out the

whites of her eyes. It was enough to see she was as confused as he was. What was happening?

BANG.

And then Evan knew. He had probably known from the first moment, but couldn't believe it. It wasn't possible.

SLAM...

"Move!" He jumped out of his hiding spot, grabbing Listings and pulling her into the center aisle with him. She didn't resist, her body limp against his. That was good. If she had fought him she would have been hit.

The shelves – the huge units they'd just been hiding behind, along with who knew how many pounds of boxes – crashed down. Driven over like two tall dominoes.

The crashing continued, each shelving unit slamming into the one behind it, tossing the contents of the evidence room to the floor in a jumbled mess.

Evan didn't know how it could be happening. It wasn't possible. It *couldn't* –

"That woulda killed us," said Listings. Something was clicking at her side, and he realized it was her gun, rattling against a button on her jeans. She was shaking.

"I think that was the idea."

He looked into the darkness, toward the front of the room. The shelves were piled on top of one another, parallel lines of chaos.

And something moved. A dark figure. Brown hair, a black coat.

The killer laughed. The same mad laugh he had laughed in the bar, the same lunatic giggle Evan had heard in the alley. It was a maggot, driving deep into the meat of Evan's brain. Feeding on him. Growing within him.

"If at first you don't succeed," said the killer.

And then he ran away. Disappeared into the darkness. His footsteps were silent.

Listings was after him in a flash. Moving so fast she was barely more than the hint of a shadow, leaping over the scattered contents of the shelves, then into the darkness as well.

"Listings, wait!"

She didn't listen.

He ran after her. Ran after both of them. Knowing he was not as fleet of foot as his partner, suspecting that neither of them had any hope of catching a man who could do all this.

(*"How do you kill a man who's already dead?"*)

Evan made it to the front of the evidence room, through the cage that hung wide open. There was no duty officer in sight. No trace of violence either. The man simply wasn't there. Something about that fact made Evan's stomach twist.

Footsteps drew his attention and he saw Listings pounding up a short flight of stairs. He ran after her. Up the stairs. Panting like he'd been running for hours. Blood drumming thunderously in his ears.

Through the doorway at the top of the stairs.

Into a hall. First floor of the building.

Cops moved through the hall, drones in the bureaucratic hive, trying to get the paperwork done and filed and triple-signed so they could get on to the "real" part of police work. Heads down, just trying to get it done and move on.

Listings stood in the middle of it all, whirling from side

to side. Looking this way, then that.

No sign of the killer.

"Dammit!" she shouted.

She started moving toward one end of the hall, clearly planning on tearing the building down one room at a time. Evan managed to put himself in her path. "Listings," he said. "Stop. He could have gone anywhere. Or nowhere."

Listings jerked, blinking in surprise at his last words. "What the hell does that mean?"

"Just...." Evan paused, wondering if he could answer that question.

Only that's wrong. You know the answer. You just don't want to admit it. The reality is too terrifying.

How do you kill a man who's already dead?

How do you?

"Let's get somewhere we can make that call," he said.

Listings nodded slowly. She wasn't shaking anymore. Fear had turned again to rage. "I'm gonna kill him. Like, infinity times."

Evan tried to smile at her. "Okay, I'll let the other kids on the playground know." The sally didn't cheer her. It didn't make him feel any better, either, so he started walking toward the other end of the hall. "Come on, Listings."

She stood still a moment longer, then followed him. She holstered her sidearm, cursing under her breath. "This is wrong. *Everything's* wrong."

She knows.

You know.

You both just have to admit it.

Evan didn't say what he was feeling. Instead he just

nodded. "I know," he said. It was all he could manage.

It would have to do.

He felt cold.

LOOPED

Flickers....

Lines, parallel, then crossing, then running away from one another....

Bits of an arm. A knife. A face.

Geist could almost see it.

It was all there. All there in the tape, in the scene that kept replaying over and over before his eyes and in his mind.

He couldn't stop watching it.

A part of his brain, a part that had fled before the all-encompassing obsession brought by the video, screamed at him to stop. Screamed at him that he didn't want to know, that he *couldn't* know.

Geist ignored the voice. It sounded like his voice, it *was* his voice. But he ignored it. He listened instead to the other voices. The ones that whispered to him of murder, of blood, of madness that would last forever and ever and cover him like the softest layer of snow until he died in smiling sleep.

Murder, blood, madness, death.

Only murder was a kind of death, wasn't it? So the beginning and end were the same.

Just like the tape. It began where it ended, and ending it simply began again. Murder and death. The end and the beginning.

He realized he was mumbling. "It keeps going. Keeps going, keeps going, keeps going keeps going keepsgoingkeepsgoingkeepsgoing...."

His voice dissolved into meaningless sounds, shadows of words. The lines and shapes of the monitor broadened, and he felt his nose touch the glass as he leaned in as close as he could. He wanted to be *part* of the scene. To see what was behind the distortion. To see the truth.

(*Don't do it! that part of him shrieked. The lie is all that lets us survive!*)

He felt someone behind him. A presence. He could vaguely see a dark shape in his peripheral vision. A swish of black, like a long coat.

Geist didn't move away from the screen. Instead he pressed harder. Pressed into it, pushed himself into the monitor, into the screen, into the scene, into the *truth*. He heard something crackle almost delicately. It was the sound of snow underfoot, the sound of Christmas presents being unwrapped.

The sound of his nose breaking as he pushed his face further into the screen.

His nose flattened. He kept pushing. Kept mumbling through the blood that flowed into his mouth.

"*Keepsgoingkeepsgoingkeepsgoing....*"

More cracks, more crinkling snaps. No longer just his nose, but his cheekbones shifting. Shattering. Harder to move his mouth now, but he kept whispering his prayer, his hope and his fear.

"*Keepsgoingkeepsgoing....*"

Then he saw. The distortions disappeared behind a curtain of his own blood. The red mixed with the whites and grays and blacks, and suddenly... he... *knew*.

He yanked himself away from the monitor. Pain blazed in his face, pain that had been there for some time now but which he hadn't noticed. The outline of his face was still on the monitor screen, painted in blood like a gruesome death mask prepared by a society that lived and died against a backdrop of technology.

He turned around. There was a man behind him. Not too tall, not too short. Just medium. Brown medium hair, a black coat.

The man Evan was looking for.

Geist knew it was. Knew it just as he knew what was happening.

"I know," he whispered. The words came out mushy. A tooth fell from his mouth. "I know *all this*."

The man – the killer – looked down on him. His eyes blazed with insanity. Then the mad candle flickers in his eyes died for a moment, and there was only pity.

Somehow that was worse.

"It doesn't matter," said the killer. "Knowing never helped anyone."

Geist tried to scream as the killer raised a knife. He couldn't. His mouth wasn't working right.

The knife fell. Geist felt it enter him. Felt it tear through him, tearing what he understood apart in white-hot flashes of pain.

He didn't shy away from it. The pain was a blessing, because it hid what he had realized. The pain smothered reality, it obscured the visions of what he had seen behind the distortions. The agony was delight, because in it he found oblivion.

And oblivion was sweet.

ECLIPSED

They were just around the corner from the station building: far enough to be able to talk freely, but close enough that Listings felt like she had a bit of a tether to reality. That was important. Because right now everything had gone so far sideways she felt like she was trying to breakdance on the side of a cliff.

That they were outside the station was weird in itself: with only one major exception she could think of, Evan had always been a stickler for the rules. So he should have been insisting they report what happened in the evidence room, and stick around to deal with the mountain of paperwork that would have to be filled out and filed.

Instead, he had the planner he had lifted from the case file – another major rule violation – and was flipping through it again. No sign he intended to go back to the station building and deal with clean-up, no sign he cared about *anything* but that planner.

Listings paced. "We are so boned. When they find the evidence room like that, we are so boned." Evan didn't seem to hear her. "You hear me, White?"

Still no trace of a response. She knocked the planner out of his hands. It landed in a puddle.

Now Evan noticed her. "Hey!"

"You do realize our careers are toilet-bound, right?"

Evan was in her face, closer than he'd ever gotten except when they were making out or making love. *"I DON'T*

CARE!"

The outburst caught her utterly by surprise, and it seemed to do the same to him. He just stared at her, and she realized she had a fist halfway cocked. No shock there: she'd always been one to start a fight faster than she could think about whether it was a good idea or not.

The shock was that Evan looked like he might actually punch her *back*.

He didn't, though. He stepped back instead, and picked up the planner. "Sorry," he mumbled. "I just don't know what's happening, Listings."

"Bad mojo," she said.

He looked up at her so sharply she heard his neck pop. "What?"

"Something my gramma used to say." She shrugged. "Funny old coot."

Evan looked away, turning the pages on the planner again, but this time moving oh-so-slowly. Using the movement to control the pace of the conversation, to get things back under control. If anyone else had tried that crap, Listings would have pounced all over him. But Evan got away with it. He got away with a lot with her.

"Listings," he finally said, "if you want to go, that's fine. I'll tell Geist the evidence room was my doing. That you were nowhere near it. I'll take the hit for it."

She considered it. Only for a half-second, but for that half-second it was a tempting thought. Then she shook her head. "Sure. You'd end up crapping into a bag when he was done tearing your ass off. Not to mention he'd fire you."

"I don't care."

Listings peered at Evan. "You mean it." He nodded.

She thought about walking away. A bit longer this time: maybe three-quarters of a second. "I'm not gonna abandon my partner. Not even if he was terrible in the sack. Which you aren't."

Evan grinned, and she felt like the sun was shining again after a night that had lasted far too long.

And, being, her, she couldn't let that be. She had to squash it. "But I need to know: what's going on, White? You're usually Mr. Rules, so what's got you so spooked that you're willing to let go of a promising career in the ass-crack of the nation?" Then, being her, she had to make it harder on herself than on anyone. "Is it Val? Still?"

Evan's smile disappeared. Not like the sun behind a cloud, but like a solar eclipse that no one could predict. "Yes. No. I don't know."

When he said, "Yes," her heart felt like someone drove over it with a big rig. The follow-up words almost disappeared in the aftermath. It took her a moment to realize he had stopped flipping the pages of the planner and was looking at her intensely.

"Listings, our marriage wasn't doing well for a long time before I found out... what she was doing." He looked down again, then back up at her. Like he was forcing himself to say something. Not something painfully bad, but something painfully good. "You don't have to worry about competition from Val. I never would have wanted it to end the way it did, but I thank God every day that it brought you and me together."

He wasn't smiling, but the sun was back. She smiled for them both. "You are such a *pussy*," she said.

Evan nodded. Shrugged. "One of us has to be in touch

with their – oof!"

The last sound was the sound a person had to make when either hit by a car or by a patent-pending Listings-hug-and-kiss-combo. She hugged him hard, kissed him harder, and he was gracious enough to pretend not to notice her wiping a few tears off her cheeks when they parted.

"Make the call before I change my mind," she said, pointing at the planner.

"You won't. I'm too good in the sack."

He smiled.

Listings felt good. Maybe this wasn't the correct move, but it was the right one.

The sun was out.

But even as she thought that, she heard his words in her mind: "I never would have wanted it to end the way it did."

She had seen Val. Throat cut, stabbed twenty-three times. The memory would never leave her.

And the investigation, the investigation she had been a part of, had helped run... it had ended up in the cold files. A failure. She would never forget that, either.

The sun was out, but a shadow lingered, always there. Always waiting to swallow the warmth and cast away the light.

WRONG

Val's Day-Timer said "House" on one of the pages. And that was something that Evan would have wondered about, if he had ever seen it. But he hadn't. It was her list of numbers, and he didn't really know what was in it. He trusted her, he always had.

He wondered how many other couples were like that: living in utter trust, never knowing the secrets the other carried in plain sight.

Under the word was the number. The one that he didn't recognize. He knew the others, either because he recognized the names above them or in the vaguely familiar way that we reserve for things that matter to someone important to us, but which are of no great importance to us. Things like the birthday of a friend of a friend, or the life facts of a character in a parent's favorite book. Things that we recognize when seen, if only dimly.

The number was alien to him. But it still made his nerves sing like he was standing on a subtly electrified surface.

He dialed it.

And she answered. On the second ring Tuyen picked up and said, "Hello?" in a voice that he would have been able to pick out in a New York subway at rush hour.

"Why is your name in my dead wife's phone book?" he said.

Dead silence fell over the line. He would have thought

she terminated the call, only he hadn't heard any click or beep.

"We should talk," she said.

"We're talking now."

"In person. Somewhere safe." Her voice trembled. She was truly terrified, he could hear it. And he didn't think it was an act, either. Years of talking to witnesses and perpetrators had given him a sense of who was lying, who was trying to play him.

Tuyen might *be* trying to play him. But she wasn't lying. She might be showing what she felt for effect, but the feelings were real.

"Why? What are you afraid of?"

The young woman laughed, sounding a bit hysterical. The laugh made his nerves stop singing. Now he felt hollow inside. Moving toward inevitable doom.

Leave this alone.

But he knew he wouldn't.

"What am I afraid of?" she said. "So many things, Mr. White."

He decided to avoid the subject of her fear. For now. Later he could ease into it. First things first, he thought. Get a meeting, find out what she knows about Val.

"Where do you want to meet –" he began.

Listings had been listening to his side of the conversation. Her phone rang. She picked up. Turned away a bit and said, "Listings" with her usual on-the-job brusqueness.

"Seven o'clock," said Tuyen. "St. Mary's on Barrow Street."

Evan knew the place. A Catholic church, a fairly large one considering it was in a part of the city that was less in need of cleaning up than a tactical nuke.

"Fine," he said. Tuyen hung up so he turned to Listings. She was nodding at whoever was on the other end of her call, something Evan always thought was weird, even though he knew he did it as well: facial expressions and gestures for people who weren't even there. It was like watching a twenty-first century séance.

"You got it," said Listings. She hung up. "That was Geist," she said. "He wants us to meet him."

"Where?" said Evan.

Listings told him, but he was barely listening. Because at the mention of Geist's name he felt his stomach clench. Like he was on a rickety ride at a carnival that hadn't passed inspection, and now the thing was getting ready to explode right under him. It was a mixture of full-tilt power and uncontrolled velocity. A sense that he was moving fast, that the screws were all coming loose.

That the world was about to tumble to pieces around him.

TERROR

Listings flicked the light switch in the A/V room. Up, down, up, down. The rattle-tap of the plastic irritated her, because it did nothing. The room stayed dark.

She was almost glad. She fed the irritation. Stoked it like an ember, blowing it to a slow-burning flame of anger that would sustain her through the fear that had gripped her since Geist asked them to meet him here. That grew when they saw the still-deserted evidence locker.

"I have something to show you," Geist had said. "Something important." And it *was* him, she was sure of it. But at the same time, he sounded wrong. Gone was his usual cheerfulness, the sound of a man who ate-drank-slept at the feet of his work and found immense joy in the doing of it.

He sounded *haunted*.

One more up-down, and she slammed her fist into the wall hard enough to dent it. "I get that we can't hire a competent mayor, but you'd at least think the taxpayers could shell out for an electrician."

"Captain?" said Evan. He moved into the small room, poking around the equipment. Listings followed, but even in the near-complete darkness it didn't take long to verify that they were alone.

Evan turned to her. He looked thin. Not physically, but emotionally. He looked like a rubber band that some kid had been snapping too long, and now was cracked and on the verge of breaking. "He's not here," he said. "You sure he said to come down –"

"Yeah," Listings said. The small fire was still there, burning away the fear but also singeing at the edges of good feelings. She snapped the word. Would have kept on snapping, maybe started an argument right there, but something interrupted her.

Light.

A flash, a bright flare.

The monitor. The television screen that Evan and then Geist had been watching.

It sparked. Then turned on.

Evan looked at her. She wondered if she looked as freaked out as he did.

Evan went to the carrel where the equipment was. She pulled out her phone, thinking she would dial Geist and find out where he was. If they knew that then all this was moot, and –

(*and then they could ignore the impossible thing that just happened, the impossible things that were* going *to happen*)

– they could go find him. But as soon as she had her phone in hand she remembered: "Dammit. No signal down here."

"Listings."

Evan was gesturing for her to look at the TV screen. Static showed, black and white pixels crawling across one another like electronic amoebae vying for dominance.

It illuminated something on the screen. She couldn't make it out at first. It was red.

The VCR hummed and clicked. The distortion from the Mystix security tape appeared again. Just as unnerving and somehow unnatural as before.

And now she saw what the red stuff was. Blood. It looked almost like a mask on the screen.

"Who turned on the tape?" she said. Praying Evan had done it without her noticing.

"I don't know," he said. The VCR was a front-loading model and he poked a finger through the light plastic cover, feeling inside. She didn't know what he was looking for. Then he spoke, and she understood: "And there *is* no tape. It's empty."

The fire burned away. Only cold ash remained. Fear.

Then the distortions on the TV disappeared, and fear was replaced by terror.

WATCHING

The screen was only clear for a moment. But that moment was long enough for Evan. Long enough, and far too long.

Val appeared. She was screaming, though no sound came from the television.

The image jumped, and a scarlet knife was in a bloody hand, falling and rising and falling and rising, like a silver phoenix born not of fire but of flesh.

He saw his wife's stomach ripped open by the blade, and felt his own stomach turn inside out.

Then the image disappeared. Evan realized he was crying.

"Val," he sobbed.

The screen had returned to its distortions, the waves that hid so much – so much that he didn't want to see.

They parted again.

"Geist!" shouted Listings.

It was. On the monitor, the captain could be seen in the A/V room, watching the same TV that Evan and Listings now watched. Leaning in close, touching the screen with his face. And on *that* television, the one he was watching, there was another image of the captain. Also pressed against the same TV, also watching, that screen also holding an image of himself. A television in a television, a captain watching a captain watching a captain in a loop that got smaller and smaller until it disappeared in a distant spot on infinity's horizon.

Beside Evan, Listings whispered, "What's going on, White?"

Evan couldn't speak. He shook his head, but had no words. Understanding had no place in something like this. Reality had fled, and – he was realizing – might never return again. So what place had logic in the dark fantasy land where they now lived?

On the monitor, all the Geists pressed into the screen. Awful cracking sounds came out of the TV speakers, amplified and resounding with feedback as the sounds battled for dominance.

Blood dripped around the edges of the many faces of Geist. So much blood. He didn't move.

"I see it all," said Evan's friend. His voice – voices – echoed in the A/V room. "I... understand...."

Then Listings jumped as something else came into the frame of each of the infinite televisions. A hand, holding a knife.

"I... understand...," said the Geists.

"Then it's time for you to die," said a voice. Evan knew the voice. The killer.

The knife raised.

"No!" Evan shouted, and reached for the television, as though he might push through the screen and stop what was about to happen.

The knives fell.

Again.

Again.

Geist was turned into a bloody puppet, along with all

his copies, each doppelganger dancing in perfect synchronization. The knife/knives plunged into him/them over and over, blood splashing the screen of the television, the carrel, the rest of the equipment.

And Geist never moved. Never turned his face from the screen. He sagged, but kept his gaze pinned to the screen as long as he could.

Then, finally, he fell. Blood surrounded him in a black pool on the carpet. Evan automatically looked at his feet.

Nothing. The floor below them was clean. Unmarked.

He returned his attention to the screen.

The killer turned to whatever camera had recorded all this. Looking right at Evan and Listings.

"Take a good look at the man who killed your wife, Evan," he said. He laughed.

The distortion returned to the television, hiding his image. Then the monitor turned off, leaving Evan staring at nothing but the faded reflections of Listings and himself. Listings' face was so bloodless it seemed to shine in the hazy glass of the screen. She weaved on her feet, and he reached for her, steadying her. She was warm. He clung to her, to her warmth, to the fact that she was here and real and something he could touch.

He needed that. Because he thought he was starting to understand. More than that, to believe. And some beliefs were by their nature not just terrifying, but deadly.

HAUNTING

Listings turned toward the door. Or maybe she turned away from the screen. Probably it was the latter. She had to get away from here, had to get away from the impossible thing she had just seen. This was no rape, no murder. This wasn't even a father being torn limb from limb by a demon in human form.

This was....

She had no words.

She didn't know what to do, but knew she had to get out of here. She had to find someone to do something. She chafed under the quasi-military structure of the police force sometimes, but right now she wanted – desperately *needed* – to find someone to whom she could pass this buck.

Evan grabbed her. "Where're you going?" he said.

She tried to pull away. "To get someone!" she said. Her voice sounded like that of a child, the voice of an Angie who had never seen her daddy murdered. An Angie who never had to be tough, never had to kill anyone. An Angie who needed to get *away*.

Evan yanked her toward him. "It won't help."

Listings tried to shake free again. Evan's fingers clamped down tighter. "What do you –"

He jerked her over. Violently this time. He looked mad, and she wondered if he was going to hit her. The prospect terrified her. What if Evan ceased to be the man he had always been? What if Val's death really *had* changed him?

Of course it did. How could that not have changed him?

Evan pointed at the floor. "You said he called. Geist *just called.*"

Listings didn't understand. She pushed him with her free hand. "So let go and maybe we can get someone to help us catch this sonofabitch!"

"If he just called, then this guy killed the captain and made an *impossible* video of it and cleaned up an entire corpse's worth of blood in under ten minutes."

Listings shook her head. She didn't want to hear this. Didn't want to see any more of what she was seeing, didn't want to know any more of what threatened to make itself known to her.

She wanted to curl up in her father's arms and sleep. Even if he was dead. Even if that meant she had to die. She just wanted to stop this.

"So he's still close," she whispered. "He's close. We can –"

Evan shook her. Hard. "Don't you get it, Listings?" He looked at the blank monitor. It flared to life for a moment, as though it had been waiting for their attention.

The captain's blood, illuminated by the static, was gone. As if it had never been.

I've gone nuts.

Then Evan's crazy, too.

Oh, Jesus, please, God, please, don't let us be crazy.

Daddy, where's your arm?

"Don't you get it Listings?" said Evan again. His voice was low in the darkness, but still cut through her. "This isn't a murder case." He took a breath, as if gathering himself.

NO! Don't say it!

(*"You can't kill a man who's already dead."*)

"It's a haunting."

Listings shook her head. But she knew it wasn't a gesture of disbelief, it was a gesture of refusal. It was the body language of someone presented with proof of truth that went against the lies they preferred to live. It was the same thing she had done when she realized her daddy was already dead, and she hadn't been able to say "I love you" one last time.

"No," she said in the same Angie-voice. "There's something going on here, but it's not –"

"We shot him, Listings. Point blank, right in the chest. And he's still here. Still killing people."

Evan slumped a bit. She tore free. "I'm calling this in. I'm –"

"You're what?" Evan didn't grab her again. He suddenly sounded exhausted, like he hadn't slept in a million lifetimes. "You're going to tell someone that we have a murder with no body, no suspect, no killer? Show them a tape that doesn't exist on a monitor that turns on when it wants to? You going to report that to our superior?" He laughed without a trace of irony. "Oh, wait. He's dead, too."

Listings felt like crying. "What are we going to do?"

Evan looked at the monitor again. So did she.

It remained dark. Just a blind eye, looking at everything, understanding nothing.

CHURCH

Evan stood in the back of St. Mary's looking for Tuyen, wondering what she could possibly do to shed light on what was happening. Worrying that any light shed would only illuminate monsters that had remained safely hidden... and were better left unseen.

The church was fairly typical. Though not huge as some of the cathedrals downtown, it still managed to impress. It was laid out in the traditional cruciform pattern, with pews extending up the nave and out the transepts – the wings of the building that Evan thought of as the arms of the cross.

He and Listings stood in the vestibule, next to several confessionals. Stations of the Cross could be seen, lining the walls of the nave and extending partly into the vestibule itself, each represented by a brass plaque showing a scene from Christ's walk to Golgotha. His face was agonized in many.

Above the stations, stained-glass windows showed biblical scenes. No doubt bright and cheery during the day, they were now dark and grim. The pictures they painted were not hopeful, but seemed to Evan like grim reminders that all light must fade, all color must dim and die.

At the front of the nave was the sanctuary and altar. An organ and choir loft to one side, the pulpit where the priest would deliver sermons opposite.

Red votive candles flickered, casting everything in dim tones that made Evan think of the crime scenes he had investigated over the years. The murders. The blood.

Listings moved beside him. She dipped the fingers of

her right hand in a small marble font filled with water. Then she knelt quickly and genuflected.

Of all that had happened in the last day or so, this might be the thing that surprised Evan the most.

Listings didn't look up as she said, "What? A girl can't kick ass and still believe?" Then she crossed herself again and said, "Sorry about the ass comment, God." She flicked a wicked grin in Evan's direction. "A girl like me *needs* church: I've probably got more to repent about than most. Some of it has to do with you."

Evan felt a blush crawl up the back of his neck. He wasn't a particularly believing person, but his parents had both been church-goers. His aunt had been a devout Catholic, in fact, which was why the setup of this place was so familiar to him. And having Listings make half-veiled single entendres in a house of God made him feel like apologizing to someone.

Evan looked away from her and checked out the pews. No mass was being held, so there were only a few people – mostly devout-looking older women dressed in dark tones – sitting in the wood seats.

The one exception was easy to find. A rainbow off to the left.

"Come on," said Evan.

He and Listings walked up the center aisle, then moved to the side. He sat next to Tuyen and Listings took up position behind the Vietnamese woman. She was praying, her head down, silent and still.

Evan waited a moment, then said. "I didn't peg you for a Catholic."

"I'm lots of things," said Tuyen. She didn't open her

eyes. "Vietnam has been invaded many times. We learn to adapt." She crossed herself and stood.

Listings half-stood as well. "Whoa, where you going, Lady Gaga?"

Tuyen looked at Listings, and Evan could tell that there was an immediate and very mutual dislike between the two women. "Somewhere safer," said Tuyen.

She walked to the front of the nave. Around the side of the altar and up a ramp that led behind it to an open door at the very back of the building.

Evan followed, looking at Listings to see if she was as surprised as he was. Tuyen didn't seem like the kind of person a priest would let just go into the church sacristy at will, but apparently she could. No one made a sound as she went through the doorway.

Evan went after her, Listings close behind. He barely heard his partner, their footsteps muffled on the thick carpet that blanketed the area around the altar.

The sacristy was the priests' chambers. Vestments hung from the walls, silver candle holders and other objects that would be used in the mass were carefully stacked on a table. A desk lamp was the only illumination.

Tuyen stood before another open door, a dark hole that allowed sight only of a few steps going down.

Evan felt strange moving into this place. Believer or not, his upbringing demanded that he respect it as a private spot if not a sanctified one.

"Are we supposed to be here?" he said.

Tuyen nodded. "Father John is a friend. He won't mind." She turned and walked down into the darkness below the sacristy.

Evan looked at Listings again. She stared at him through eyes that seemed less hard-bitten than usual. She was nervous. Scared.

Evan had never thought he would encounter something that would truly scare her.

He turned away before the sight killed his ability to move. He followed Tuyen down into darkness.

NAMES

When Tuyen saw the man's outline through the shop window, she worried.

When she saw her offerings defiled, she feared.

When the policeman called, she understood.

And that... that was the worst of all.

Now she stood, arms crossed, her back against the cold marble of the crypt below the sacristy. It was a burial place for important members of the congregation, dating back over two hundred years, to the time when St. Mary's had first been erected. The church itself had been lost to fire, rebuilt, torn down and rebuilt again.

But the crypt had remained.

It was nothing grotesque, nothing out of a horror film or a nightmare. It was comforting. Cool marble, with inscriptions and age-darkened plaques along some of the walls. No one had been interred here in decades – modern regulations wouldn't permit it – but the righteous dead of old were here. That made Tuyen feel better. And, she hoped, it afforded a measure of protection.

Detective White came down first. He looked around, clearly understanding what the place was, just as clearly shocked to see it. But he didn't say anything. Tuyen liked him. He seemed like a good man.

The woman came next. Tuyen did *not* like her. She looked around, too, and Tuyen could see fear in her eyes. The woman didn't know what was happening. Or maybe she *did* know, at least a little. Either way, she was scared. And fear mixed with something in lady cop's past and came out as anger.

"Why was your name in his wife's planner?" she demanded, pointing at Detective White.

"I cleaned for her."

The lady frowned. "I thought you worked at the hoodoo shop."

Irritation whittled away some of the sharp edges of Tuyen's fear. "Not everyone can afford to survive on one job, lady. And it's not voodoo."

The woman took a step toward her, like she was going to scold her or maybe just beat her to death.

Detective White stopped her. "How come I never saw you at my house?" he said in a quiet voice.

He was listening. More than that, he was ready to believe. Tuyen would talk to him. She had learned long ago that it was useless to try to convince people of anything. The more important something was to them, the less likely they were to change their ideas.

But if they came to you. If they *asked* for your help, and trusted your answers... then truth could be given.

She thought how to answer him, deciding finally that being kind would take too long. She didn't know how much time they all had. "You never saw me for the same reason you never saw your wife's boyfriend."

She saw him wince. Maybe that was too far. "Sorry," she said. "I've been coming for a long time. Cleaning a few times a week, just an hour or two here and there. One day I came early, and... I found them. I had never seen you in person, but I knew she was married. She threatened me."

Tuyen frowned. She remembered the day, the cold woman speaking to her as though she were a child to be bullied. "I didn't like that. So next time I saw them together...."

She let the words hang. Detective White understood. "You were the one who called me home that day. Not my wife, *you* sent that message!"

Tuyen nodded. She looked away. "I wanted to get her back. And besides, it was wrong what she was doing."

"Did you kill Val?" asked the lady cop. She looked at Tuyen intensely, then at Detective White, and Tuyen realized how much he must have been wondering the same thing.

"Listings –" began Detective White.

"No!" Tuyen almost shouted it. "Two policemen came and asked me about that already. I had an alibi. I was working at the shop, at Mystix." She stepped a bit closer to Detective White. It was important that he understand the truth. That he believe her. "You know who did it," she said.

Detective White stood still. He looked like he was having a fight with himself, a terrible struggle going on inside. Tuyen couldn't fault him for that: it was terrible to have to admit that the unreal is real, that the things we have been taught are wrong and that our nightmares have become flesh.

"The guy from the bar," said the lady cop.

Tuyen nodded. "I've seen him, too. He's been following me. Been in my house, took some of my charms."

"How?" demanded the lady cop. Listings. "How is he doing all this."

Tuyen didn't bother answering her. She wasn't ready to believe yet, and Tuyen wasn't going to waste breath trying to convince her.

Listings drew her own conclusions from Tuyen's silence. She shook her head. "Come on, Pink. I need more than vague –"

"He's dead, isn't he?" said Detective White.

Tuyen nodded.

Listings' jaw dropped open so far Tuyen expected it to bounce off her boobs. It would have been funny if it wasn't all so terrible. *"What?"* she said to Detective White. "Have you and Katy Perry here lost your minds?"

Detective White ignored her, which made Tuyen like him more. "So shouldn't he be...." He gestured around them. The names of the pious on the walls. "An angel or something?"

Tuyen shook her head. She heard Gramma's words in her mind, almost as though the old woman had come back to tell her what to say. "Death doesn't grant wings to the wicked." She looked at the two cops, hoping to see the strength they would all need. And realizing that whether it was there or not, they were the people who would have to fight this fight.

"My grandmother was from the old country," she said. "She taught me there are three kinds of *bong ma*. Of ghosts." She held out a finger for each, counting down to the most dangerous. "First are ghosts who have unfinished business. Those are the ones you most hear about. They're afraid to go beyond the veil without seeing their work done." Another finger went out. "The saddest are the ones who are stuck in a loop, replaying the last scenes of their lives over and over, never able to influence the world, never quite understanding what's going on." She paused, then the third finger speared out. "Worst are the vengeful spirits. People who should have gone to Hell, but whose anger keeps them anchored to the earth." She looked at her fingers. Dropping all but the third. "Guess which one we've got."

Silence.

Finally, Detective White said, "How do we stop him?"

Listings repeated her jaw-drop. "Seriously?" The cop looked like she couldn't decide whom to yell at, finally turning on her partner. "White, this guy is just some nut. He's clever, he's got some new tricks, but he's flesh and blood and we can catch him." Her voice started to lose strength at the end of her tirade, and Tuyen still saw the fear that lay over her spirit like a blanket of snow.

Tuyen had always had the sight. Sometimes she didn't want it. Sometimes she saw wrong. But she always saw.

Detective White must have seen it, too. "Really?" he said. "Then explain to me what's happening. Geist. The evidence room. Televisions that turn on and off on their own. A guy who takes a chest full of bullets without bleeding and then disappears into thin air!"

His voice got louder where hers had softened. Listings almost shrank before him. Sometimes truth did that. It was part of what made seeing things so dangerous. Truth was heavy, and could crush some people out of existence.

Detective White turned to Tuyen. "What do we do?"

Tuyen leaned back against the wall again. Clutching herself so tightly that she could feel her own fingers drawing bruises up against the skin of her arms. "Not many places are safe," she said. "Here, with the souls of the saved. Maybe at the shop."

Detective White slashed through the air with the flat of his hand. "I don't care about safe. How do we fight him? How do we *kill* him?"

Listings, watching them both as they spoke, retreated from fear back to anger again like a child running home. "You go ahead and keep on chatting with Rainbow Brite," she said to Detective White. "I'll be upstairs with the living and the sane."

She turned away.

"You believe," said Tuyen.

Listings stopped. "What?"

"I saw you when you came in the church. You believe."

"Not in this."

"Why not?"

For a moment Tuyen thought she had reached the lady cop. That she hadn't just wasted her breath. Listings turned around and Tuyen thought she saw the real person under the woman's armored gaze. She looked suddenly like a little girl.

"Why believe in one miracle and not in another?" said Tuyen.

"Because one gives me hope," said the little girl version of the lady cop. "And the other scares the hell out of me."

Then she ran out of the crypt, disappearing up the stairs.

Tuyen pushed away from the wall. She didn't like the lady, but she understood suffering. She understood having your world turn upside down, having the things you loved stripped from you.

Detective White shook his head. "Let her go. You

have to let her work through it when she's like this, or the only thing that happens is you end up with fewer teeth." He sighed, the sound of someone grappling with emotions he couldn't quite control.

"Is there a way to stop this guy? Or thing, or whatever he is?" he finally said.

Tuyen nodded. "Ghosts have names. Speaking the name of a ghost is the only way to stop them, to hurt or even touch them if they don't want to be touched." She caressed one of the names on the wall, an inscription so faded with the many lingering traces of loved ones' hands that the letters had nearly been wiped away. "To be a ghost is to be locked in a lie, and only truths have power over them."

"Do you know this one's name?"

The marble hadn't changed under Tuyen's fingers, the air around her was the same. But she felt cold.

"Do you think I'd be cowering down here if I did?"

The letters under her fingers *were* gone. She couldn't read them. The air was cold. Death surrounded them.

And she could not see if it had come to protect, or take them.

She shivered.

LIES

Listings had lied.

When the others were talking about ghosts and death giving wings to the wicked, Listings said it wasn't true. That they were insane.

But it *was* true. And it was the world that was insane.

She knew it was true, and probably had known for a while. Had known since the day her father died: after all, if a demon could come into her house and kill her angel, then it made sense that others would walk the darkness. Not just muggers and rapists and murderers, but things of pure evil. Things that converted the world into a cage, a place where humanity had been thrown not as children to play, but as meat for the beast.

She ran from it. Ran from it, and from her lies.

So many lies.

Too many.

She ran up the steps, but the lies followed her. And it wasn't just her denials in the crypt. It was all the lies. All of them.

She ran into the sacristy. She hoped it might offer her comfort, being in the private places of the priests, the spots where final prayers were uttered before masses were offered and sermons given.

She found no comfort. Instead, she found hands.

They snatched at her, encircled her throat.

She tried to scream, but the air was utterly cut off. She

had seen so many movies where people choked each other, offering out tiny croaks, little noises that summoned others. It was crap. If you were being choked – *really* choked – no noise came. None at all.

Just like now.

She looked at the man choking her. The brown hair and brown eyes that seemed so normal, until you looked a bit deeper. Until you saw the fires behind them, the flames that had burned away his sanity.

And as darkness closed around her vision, folded over her and covered her, she realized that the flames weren't madness. They were *truth*.

The killer wasn't one of those who had gone crazy to hide from reality. He had gone mad because of the truths he had seen.

Listings thought about her lies.

She wondered for an instant if they had protected her.

She felt a hand leave her throat.

Something sharp pierced her.

The lies flowed out of her.

The darkness came in.

PREPARATIONS

"So… we don't know his name, so we're screwed? We just let him knock us off or do whatever it is he's going to do?"

Tuyen didn't answer Evan's question right away, and he started to wonder if he hadn't spoken loudly enough. Not normally something he worried about, but since everything else was so wrong, so confused, it wouldn't surprise him to be struck deaf, dumb, and blind.

He wasn't even sure he would mind. He was already running around in the dark, so it wouldn't be much of a change.

"There are things. Dangerous things." Tuyen didn't turn to him, but he heard fear digging hooks into her voice, peeling it back, flaying her soul.

She looked at Evan, one hand still on the marble of the crypt wall as if to maintain contact with something she could believe in, could find comfort in. "I'll meet you at the shop. Midnight."

Evan shook his head. "Why midnight? Why not now? We need to get this guy."

Tuyen looked away. "I need to prepare." Her voice was muffled now, and Evan had the strange sensation that if he grabbed her and swung her around he would find no face, only a fleshy expanse of skin unbroken by mouth or eyes. Speech without speaking, sight without seeing.

He swallowed. His mouth was so dry it felt like gravel scraping down his throat. "How?" he said.

Tuyen didn't speak. She put her other hand on the wall, leaning against it like a perp about to get frisked.

The lights in the crypt flickered. For a moment, the fraction of an instant between light and dark, Evan thought he saw blood on her shirt, blood on the white floor at her feet.

Then the lights came on again.

Tuyen knelt down. Hands still on the wall, she began to pray.

Evan watched her for long enough to realize that this was it, this was what she was going to do until midnight. She was going to pray.

God help him, he was going to hinge his hopes on someone whose big plan was to pray for the next few hours.

He backed away from her. She didn't move, didn't so much as twitch. She was murmuring the low, cadenced tones of a liturgical prayer. The sound went on and on and on. It was almost hypnotizing.

Evan was suddenly reminded of the lines on the security tape, the distortions that masked something terrible and true.

What's behind this?

What am I not seeing?

What's behind this?

What am I not seeing?

His body twitched, an abrupt jerk that forced him out of the circle of thoughts, yanked him back to the present. Back to the here and now.

As it did, another thought came.

Where's Listings?

SOUND

Evan ran down the steps of the church, hoping to see something, terrified he wouldn't.

"Listings!"

The steps that led to the front of the church were wide and deep, the kind of thing that had been built before Los Angeles became so crowded it became too expensive to indulge in such luxuries. They swept out to the sides, broadening as they approached the sidewalk so the last stair was a good thirty feet in length.

Evan stepped off, looking up and down the street.

The church was located in the middle of a small road. Not a main thoroughfare, not even a large avenue. Just the church, a few small buildings – mostly offices.

There was no movement.

"Listings!"

His call ricocheted off the steps, bouncing up and out before being swallowed by the night. No one answered. No one moved.

Maybe she's still somewhere in the church.

Unlikely, but he turned to run back up the steps again.

The door of the church – only visible from this angle as a short sliver of brown that seemed to sit atop the highest stair – slid shut. Evan heard it thunk solidly.

He knew from his aunt that this meant they must have closed for the night. No more mass, no more people coming in to pray or contemplate in the hopes of finding divine answers to mortal problems.

He ran the last twenty steps. It seemed to take far too long. He hammered on the door with the flat of his palm, then with the fleshy part of his fist. The door was solid, old. His hand did little more than make a wet slap. It sounded like he was beating on the side of a rock, and probably wasn't heard.

"Open up!"

He backed up as he shouted, looking around for another way in or for sign of his partner. Seeing neither.

His hand went in his pocket as he shouted, "Listings!" again. He pulled out his cell. Dialed Listings' number.

One ring.

Two.

Three.

It picked up.

"Oh, thank God –"

"We're sorry," said the oh-so-pleasant and oh-so-false voice. "The number you are trying to reach is busy or no longer in service. Please hang up and try –"

He turned the phone off and shoved it in his pocket as he ran. "Listings!"

His legs pumped fast and hard. He was barely aware of which way he chose to run. Sweat poured down his brow, his neck, pooled at the small of his back.

Sweat....

And he is *there* again. Looking at Val, writhing under her lover. Smiling at him.

He stumbles back. Away from what he sees. Away from the sounds. Away from her smile.

He trips back into the hall. His knees wobble, his feet mix up in each other and he falls. His hands fly out, but he is moving too fast in his panic, the world has been pulled out from under him far too quickly to stop his tumble into Hell.

He hits his head on the wall opposite the bedroom. The bedroom he and Val shared for so long. The bedroom he thought of not as *his* or *hers* but *theirs*.

The blow to his head makes everything shift, makes everything around him desaturate from lively colors to dead grays, as though he has been thrown back to pre-Oz Kansas. Certainly no twister could have shattered his world so thoroughly.

He is on the floor. He must have blacked out. He gets back up. Goes back through the doorway.

Val is still there. Still in the bed, still smiling.

Her lover is gone. The sliding door that leads to their small backyard is open.

Evan hears birds chirping. He wishes he could poison them all for daring to sing on this day.

Val's smile doesn't falter. Not even as she speaks. "You had to find out sooner or later," she says, and her voice holds no remorse, no guilt. She pulls the sheets up to cover herself, but it is not modesty. He knows that. She simply has no more need to pretend he has any right to look at her.

"Close the door on the way out."

Evan screams.

And, screaming…

... was back on the street. Still running, still hoping to find the one person he had left.

"Listings!" he shouted again. His voice sounded loud in the night, but the night did not answer him. It simply swallowed scream, took it into itself and hid it away among the many other cries that no doubt had been uttered in darkness, the many other secrets it no doubt kept.

Evan's phone rang.

He stopped running so fast he felt like his skeleton might just catapult right out of him, leaving him a slowly collapsing pile of meat on the sidewalk. No bones emerged, though, only his cell as he fumbled it out of his pocket.

The caller ID said one word: "Angela."

He accepted the call as the phone started to chirp again, shouting, "Listings!" before the phone was even to his mouth.

Then he felt sick inside as he heard the voice of madness on the other end of the line. "Sorry, just me," said the killer.

"Where's Listings?" Evan tried to push down the terror and sound strong. "You touch her and –"

"Shhh." The killer's voice was utterly unfazed. "Shhhhhh...." Evan wanted to keep shouting, but didn't know where he could go with his threat. Everything Tuyen had said about ghosts of vengeance and needing to speak their names and everything else had been straight-up insane. It didn't just fly in the face of the rational processes Evan had devoted his life to, it sucker punched them in a dark alley and then rifled through their pockets for the hell of it.

And still, he believed what she'd said. Believed it all.

"I'm going to return her to you," said the killer. Evan tried not to speak, worried that anything he said would provide leverage the killer could use against him or Listings. "Please go to the alley."

Evan looked to his right. There was an alley there, a black corridor into the darkest parts of the night.

"Yep, that's the one," said the killer.

Evan walked toward it. Slowly. Looking around, trying to spot his enemy. "Where are you?" he said as he stepped into the alley.

It wasn't a blind alley, no dead end like the alley behind Mystix. Nor was it full of litter and graffiti. Perhaps the presence of the church had exerted a calming influence on the otherwise excitable gangs in this area. Maybe it was simply an area that had gotten lucky so far, but would be vandalized in due course. Maybe it was something else, some unnamed force keeping this place clean and safe from defacement.

Whichever it was, the only thing on the blank walls that shot up on either side of Evan were fire escapes. Each building had one, clinging to its side like a skeletal snake, boney bodies writhing up to the twin roofs, iron ribs jutting darkly from the cement walls.

"Where are you?" Evan said again.

"Does it matter?"

Evan kept moving. His head swiveled back and forth, up and down. He let nothing pass by his notice.

But there was nothing to see.

He was still alone. Alone now more than ever, because the bastard had his partner. Had *Listings*.

"Let her go."

The night seemed suddenly silent, and beyond silent. It seemed muffled, as though the universe had inhaled and was now holding its breath. Something was going to happen.

The killer was silent as well. Not ignoring Evan, he could somehow *sense* the man on the other end of the phone, could even sense the man's smile, the confidence that drove him to some unknown and horrible destination.

Then the killer said, "I had other plans for her, but... as you wish."

There was a short, weak scream. Then a series of thuds, clanks. Flesh on metal.

Evan looked up.

"NO!"

The darkness here was not absolute, not like the alley outside Mystix. There was enough ambient light from the street, from the city itself, that he could see the black form spinning through the air. Could see arms flung out to catch nothing at all, could see legs spasming as they hit the first level of the fire escape.

Could see Listings crash down, down, down. She hit the serpentine cage of the fire escape, bounced off and pinballed across the narrow alley to the metal snake that hung across the way. Her legs hit the skeletal railing that encircled a landing. They wrapped up for a moment and Evan heard a brittle snap but he was glad, glad because he thought she would hang there. Hanging, even hanging with a broken leg, was better than the alternative.

He ran toward the ladder for that fire escape. Thinking he could get up to her. Could save her.

Metal groaned.

Listings was silent.

She fell.

Her body hit the landing below. It spun again, arms and legs now limp, bending in too many places. She flipped over to the opposite fire escape. Hit again. Bounced back. Fell straight down this time.

The impact on the ground made almost no noise at all. Like she had used up her quota of sound on the way down. Just the tiniest of thumps, a sound that was wetter than it should have been.

Evan wished, in that moment that lasted forever, that instant when he saw his partner fall to earth like an angel cast down from Heaven's highest parapets, that there *had* been noise. That the sound she made when her body hit the cement was loud enough to shatter windows and set off car alarms. Because the fact of its weakness almost seemed itself like a death sentence. Like she had used up her noise on the way down, and her last gasp of life would be represented in the low, meaty smack of impact.

Something splashed him. At first he thought Listings must have fallen in a puddle.

But no, there were no puddles in this alley. It was too clean.

No puddles.

So it wasn't water that had flung itself against his feet, against his lower legs.

He ran to her.

Praying she was alive. Praying he could save her.

COUNTDOWN

She was only a few feet away. And yet it seemed to take a long time to get to her. So long that for a few seconds/minutes/lifetimes Evan wondered if he was dreaming. This all had that nightmare quality, that feeling every human has experienced where they are caught in the grips of sleeping terror, running forever toward a goal that can never be captured, racing through air that seems thick and finally hardens around them like concrete.

I'm dreaming.

The thought was hopeful. And the hopefulness, ironically, dashed all hope. For hope could not be found in a nightmare. Hope can only be found in the midst of true tragedy. Nightmares are defined by their overwhelming despair, which becomes a caricature of itself and so has no power upon waking. But hope felt in the face of burgeoning calamity makes the shock and horror bite all the deeper when it comes.

So Evan felt hope and, hoping, despaired.

He ran the few steps to the body. One foot fell on dry asphalt, the next splashed in a puddle that was too dark and thick to be water.

The next two were dry.

Then another splash.

Another.

His pants were bloody.

The body lay at his feet. Limbs bent and broken,

shattered and crooked with too many joints.

The throat was slashed, the stomach riddled with stab wounds.

And Evan felt elation.

It's not Listings. It's Val!

His wife stares up at nothing, throat slashed, body punctured. The blue sheets twisted around her, a snake risen to fee on the carcass of the damned.

She twitches.

And Evan realizes.

No....

It wasn't Val. His memory clouded, disappeared. He wasn't looking at Val.

He was looking at his partner, his lover, his friend.

Listings spasmed again. She reached for him. Blood pooling around her, leaking from the wounds all over her body, the cuts and stabs that were exactly the same as the ones inflicted on Val.

The killer was mocking Evan with his partner's death.

Evan knelt next to her. He didn't expect her to say anything, not with a cut throat, but apparently the gash wasn't deep enough to sever her windpipe or her larynx. Listings managed a few words.

"Never... never told you," she said. Her voice was low, rough. It burbled like a brook. Lungs filling with blood, and red bubbles burst on her lips.

"Shh. Don't talk." Evan's eyes filled with tears. He expected Listings to call him a pussy for that, then realized she probably couldn't see him. She wasn't going to be saying any of those nasty, acidic, wonderful things anymore.

"Never told you I knew. Everything. How you felt." She hitched in a breath. Tried to cough. More bubbles burst. "I know it hurt. What Val did. But I was glad. Meant I had a chance." She smiled a bit. Or maybe it was just a trick of the light, a hope in Evan's heart. "More than just partners in crime."

"Hold on, Listings." He crushed her hand to him. "Stay with me, Angela."

"Angela." The smile broadened. He wasn't imagining it. "You never called me that before."

She died.

The smile was broad. And it was, somehow, the same smile as the one Val had worn.

He couldn't look at it.

He closed his eyes. Kissed her forehead. Still warm. He didn't know why that surprised him, but it did. As though the dead should cool and their memories fade in an instant. It would be better, easier.

But that wasn't reality. Reality was a dead wife, a dead mentor and friend, and now this.

His lips lingered against her forehead. He had a moment of insanity, a terrible instant where he thought about pulling out his gun and ending it here. Blowing out his brains while still kissing the warm forehead of the woman he loved, the woman who had really loved him back.

Then he realized he had a better use for his gun.

He drew back from his partner. He could look at her now. Her smile *wasn't* like Val's. Nothing like it at all.

"You always had a chance," he said.

His gun was in his hand. He didn't remember drawing it. Didn't know if he had taken it out to kill himself, or because he knew that he was going to find a way to destroy the man – or ghost, or demon, or *thing* – that had killed Listings.

And he didn't care.

Evan ran for the fire escape on his right. The ladder stretched nearly to the ground, close enough that he didn't even have to jump for it. He just reached up and began climbing. Hand over hand, barely hampered by the gun that he held.

First landing. A few steps, a sharp turn. Then he was on the steps, the iron ribs of the snake. He sprinted up the stairs, the treads clanking underfoot as he ran. He was panting by the end of the second flight. By the third his heart felt like it might explode.

He pushed himself faster. Turn, turn, turn. He circled up the spiraling steps, not looking up, not daring to look down. For a moment the stairs were all that was, like he was a hamster in a wheel, a creature that had fallen into a life-sized Mobius strip.

Then the stairs ended.

Up a short ladder, only ten rungs.

His mind returned enough that he stopped for an instant before poking his head over the rooftop.

What if the killer was just waiting for this? Waiting for Evan to poke his dumb head over the edge? Waiting to shoot him or bludgeon him or stab him? There was no way he could have missed the sound of Evan rushing up the steps.

Evan hung there for a moment, trying to listen over the

thunder-sound of his heartbeat, the hurricane of his panting.

He heard nothing. Nothing but himself. Alone in a world composed only of grief and the shattered body of his friend. Just him and memory, and that was too terrible to be borne.

So he went over. Kill or die, he couldn't stand this any longer.

Onto the roof.

The tar paper roof was coated with pebbles that crackled under his feet. It sounded like breaking bones, like the shattering of hundreds of femurs as they hung for an instant on metal railings.

He turned left and right.

Crackle, crackle.

His gun swung in front of him, leading the way, searching for the killer as much as Evan was. He could feel it, hungry for the murderer's life.

The roof was empty.

There were a few small air intakes with fans that spun in the night, aluminum blades glinting in the reflected lights of the city. A pipe or two that might house electrical conduits. Nothing large enough for a small dog to hide behind, let alone a man. There didn't even seem to be a roof access door – probably the reason the fire escape was so easy to get onto.

He was alone.

Only one way up or down: the way he had taken. No other way to get here, and no one had passed him, but *he was alone.*

Evan screamed. Rage, frustration, terror, grief. They all poured out of him in a primal cry that flew to the night sky and disappeared and left him still alone.

He screamed again, and again.

Then heard something.

Tinny, tiny laughter.

He realized that he had never turned off the cell phone. It was in his pocket. He pulled it out, jammed it against his jaw and his ear so hard that he knew he'd have a bruise there later.

The killer was laughing on the other end of the line. Giggling like a child on Christmas morning... but a terrible Christmas, and a terrible child. A kid who delighted in unwrapping his presents to find out what kind of body each box held.

"I'm not there, Evan," he said. "Not anywhere, it seems. But everywhere, all the same."

Evan's hands clenched around the phone and the gun. He turned around, whirling in every direction as though he might triangulate the killer's location. "I'm going to find you. I'm going to find you and –"

"And what? Shoot me? Kill me?" The laughter grew louder. "Please. *Please* try. I'd truly like to see that." Then the laughing stopped. Cut off as quickly as if the killer had been decapitated mid-giggle. "But not yet, Evan. Not yet. I still have one thing to take."

It seemed like a crate of daddy long-legs spiders had just been dumped down the back of Evan's shirt. Electric tingles and frozen pinpricks rode their way from the base of his skull to his tailbone. He remembered the "notes" Geist had taken before being murdered, the papers that had fallen to arrange themselves into an impossible message:

I'L KIL Evry 1 U LUv

Evan was still standing at the edge of the roof. He looked down into the alley, a dark gap between the forever-light of a city that never quite slept.

Listings was still there. Laying far below, a twisted island floating in a sea of dark blood.

He looked away. "There's nothing left to take," he said into the phone. "Nothing I love."

The killer didn't speak for a moment, as though weighing Evan's words. "Maybe. But there's one more person who helped you. Even if you don't love her, I bet it'll still bother you when I gut her."

There was a subtle electronic click. The sound of a call ending.

The sound of a countdown beginning.

GONE

Evan was back down the ladder before the words had even sunk in. Circling his way back down the snake, dialing at the same time.

The phone rang.

Rang.

Rang.

Picked up. "The number you are trying to reach is busy or no –"

Evan swore. He hung up and redialed. Halfway down the fire escape.

Same result.

He was thinking about his aunt as he dialed the third time. She was nothing like Tuyen. She was conservative, quiet, and would probably prefer death to a pierced nose.

But when she prayed, when she prayed about something important – the way Tuyen had been praying – she always closed herself off from the world. She shut the blinds. She lowered the lights.

She turned off her phone.

Evan knew that Tuyen had done the same. Knew it the same as he knew the killer was going after her next. There were things that he could just *tell*, things that he felt after years of working as a cop. Things that made sense, the same way gravity made sense. They just were, because that was the only way they *could* be.

Tuyen was in danger.

And he couldn't call her.

Still, he went to dial again as he clanked down the last set of stairs. Because maybe he'd get lucky. The world had turned inside out tonight, so maybe this instinct of his would be wrong and he'd be able to reach Tuyen, to warn her.

His fingers froze on the third digit. He never dialed the fourth.

He went down the ladder in a daze, gaze never wavering from what he had just spotted. What he *hadn't* seen.

He jumped the last six feet, landing in a spray of loose gravel, hands going to the ground and coming up black.

He looked around. Spinning again, turning around as he had on the roof. Only he wasn't looking for a killer this time. No, he was looking for something else.

"Listings?"

She was gone. Her body had disappeared.

And more than that. Even the blood had somehow been scoured from the cracked asphalt of the alley. Just like Geist, the killer had taken her. And not just taken her, but taken her so completely it was as though the world had devoured every trace of her presence, every particle of her ceasing to exist.

"Listings!"

He was screaming for a dead woman.

He knew she wouldn't answer.

Tuyen.

Tuyen is still alive.

He ran from the alley. Toward the church.

He was there in only a moment. It was dark, shut,

forbidding.

He ran up the steps, funneled toward the entrance like an insect in a pitcher plant.

Evan hammered on the door. Not just with his hands, but with the butt of his gun.

"Tuyen! Someone! Open up! Open up, dammit!"

The church remained silent. Dark.

He pulled on the door.

It did not open.

"Tuyen!"

FAITH

Tuyen's grandmother had been a tiny lady. Small to the point of being miniscule, but with a loud voice that commanded attention. Tuyen hated that sometimes, hated the fact that all too often she would come home between jobs and Gramma would say "Come in and tell me about your day" and it wouldn't be an invitation but a *command*.

But Gramma couldn't really help herself. She was a woman of Power. A woman who had come from the Old Country and made a place in a new world. She had carved out a life, had survived more danger and loss than Tuyen could even understand. So she had earned her strength, *deserved* her strength.

Still, the fact that she so thoroughly ran all life in the apartment had occasionally been a bother.

And Tuyen wished that she was here. She would give anything for Gramma to return, to provide her presence and lend her aid. Gramma had known the great secrets. She had passed many of them on to Tuyen before she died. Many, but not all.

Enough? Perhaps.

At the least, she had given Tuyen enough knowledge to be well and truly afraid.

Even here in the crypt, surrounded by saints, Tuyen felt terror clutching at her. There were ways to cast out demons, but she knew they all required one thing: faith. Real belief, true conviction.

The crosses wielded as weapons against monsters in movies were of no value in reality unless held by a hand of conviction. The charms she hoped to craft would not function unless she could bring herself to a place where she not only knew God's will, but believed in it enough to follow it.

This would be hard. "Many know all about God," Gramma often said. "Few know enough about themselves to trust Him over their own stupidity."

She often looked at Tuyen with knowing eyes when she said those things. Usually after Tuyen had just gotten a new tattoo or another piercing. Things Gramma did not approve of, because they were not in keeping with tradition, and did not show respect to the temple of her soul. On those days Gramma spoke to her with extra concern, because she was worried that Tuyen no longer believed.

She was wrong, though: Tuyen had always believed. Just as she had always seen behind the realities of life to the *truth* of things, she had always believed in God. But believing in God was far easier than *trusting* Him to save you. Than putting your life in His hands.

She suddenly felt cold, as though her body were reacting to the low point of her thoughts. She felt like she was falling into a pit of doubt, someplace dark and frozen, a place so far lost that even the fires of Hell could not find it. She hadn't moved since Detective White had left, her hands had been pressed against frigid marble walls for what seemed a lifetime.

She pulled away, feeling her joints ache. The pain was pleasant in a way. Pain was a reminder of life. That was something else Gramma had said. "Only the dead cannot feel, only the demons have no pain," she would whisper on days when her arthritis was so bad she could barely get out of bed.

But hearing Gramma's voice in her mind was different than having her here.

Believing in God was different than trusting Him to save.

Tuyen opened her eyes. For a second she wondered where she was, as everything seemed strange. Then she realized she was still in the crypt, only it appeared different to her because...

... the lights had dimmed.

She was cold.

The lights were dim.

She turned slowly. But knew. Knew before she saw.

"Did you really think this place would keep you safe?" The ghost smiled. "The spirits of the dead can't keep *me* away." He was wearing the same black coat that Tuyen had half-glimpsed through a dark window before.

Only now she saw him up close. She saw all of him, head to toe. Nothing unusual, nothing unique. He didn't glow, he didn't phase in and out of sight.

She could see him perfectly.

Her eyes widened.

"I didn't realize it was you," she said.

The ghost's forehead wrinkled in confusion so sudden and obvious it nearly appeared a parody of itself. "What?"

"I know your name," she said. And dared to smile. She found her faith. She felt Gramma close by, if not in body or spirit, then in memory. She could hear the old woman whisper, "Say it," and Tuyen knew that saying it was all she needed to do.

Still on her knees before him, but the power was hers.

She opened her mouth to say the word.

And the ghost swiped something through the air.

Tuyen spoke his name. Her mouth formed the word, the short syllables that would give her power.

But no sound came.

Instead she felt warmth flood her mouth. She gagged. Coughed. Choking. Blood.

He had cut her throat.

She saw the knife in his hand. The blade of a ghost, but solid enough to cut. Real enough to kill. It was flecked with her blood.

Arterial spray arced in front of her. It splattered the white marble walls, sprayed across the floor. It spilled down the front of her shirt, painted her breasts in a new and awful tattoo, one she never would have wished for herself.

She fell to hands and knees.

The ghost watched. He was smiling. She could *feel* his smile.

She tried to talk again. She just needed to say one word. Just one word. She would have the power if she could say his name.

She vomited blood. That was the only sound she made.

Darkness congealed at the edges of her vision. She only had seconds. She looked around for something. Anything.

There was a small table where she had put her purse and her phone. The phone was blinking: a missed call.

She wobbled toward the table on hands and knees.

Her hands started sliding in front of her. She couldn't figure out why, then realized abruptly that she was skating on a thick layer of her own still-pumping blood.

She reached for the table.

The ghost swept it aside.

The phone flew against a wall and smashed. He laughed.

The purse slammed into the wall as well. The few contents rained down on her. Not much: a few dollars, some receipts. A lipstick, a few other things.

She curled around it all.

Twitched.

The ghost, the spirit of a madman, leaned in close and licked his lips. His knife raised high.

Her fingers moved. It was all she *could* move. Her body felt empty. Her fingers were still under her control, but not for long.

The killer's knife fell. Then again, and again, and again.

It hurt at first.

Then it stopped hurting.

Then *everything* stopped.

HELD

Evan thrust his way through the bamboo screen, pushing into Mystix and hoping that he would find Tuyen there.

This had been his only option. He had to find the girl, had to ask her to shift her preparations. To find a way to get Listings back.

Listings had disappeared. She was gone. Perhaps gone wasn't the same as dead. Perhaps he could find her again.

Still, even as he swept into the shop he knew that his hope was one born of terror and madness. There was no coming back for his partner. Her body had been snatched away by the killer, but she had been dead when it happened. Lifeless and cooling in the night that cared not at all that the last person Evan loved had been stolen from him.

"Tuyen!" he shouted. "Tu –"

The second shout shattered at the edges of speech, broke into a million tiny fragments too small to hear, joining with the silence so instantly that it would have been impossible for an onlooker to tell when the scream ended and the stillness began.

He looked around and realized that the shop was different. There were no customers, no one tended the cash register.

It was dark.

"Tuyen?" he said. There was no response, and he did not expect that there would be. Evan had knocked on countless doors, cased countless businesses in his time as a cop. And he, like most of his fellows, knew that empty buildings had a feeling. Not just quiet, but a sense that the breath within them had departed. As though the inhabitants of homes or the patrons of businesses, once leaving, took with them whatever vicarious form of life the places enjoyed. To look at an empty building was to look at something truly dead, and most good cops could tell by looking at a house whether there was someone in it – even hiding – nine times out of ten. You just *felt* them. The life reaching out in your soul, touching the life in theirs. Sometimes the life was filthy and stained, sometimes the mere fact of its proximity made you feel like you needed a bath. But the sensation was a real one, and one that could be counted on in determining how hard to search an empty place.

Mystix was dead. Not just empty, but... rotten. It felt evil in here in a way that Evan didn't remember it feeling before.

With that thought, his eyes were drawn to the curtain that cut the shop in half. It seemed to weave in the darkness, though he couldn't feel any movement of air that would have caused it to roll like that. Even if there had been air conditioning or a fan, he didn't think they would have been sufficient to cause the heavy cloth to billow.

He moved to the curtain. It grew larger as he did, stretching not just from floor to ceiling but seeming to encapsulate his entire world. It was a horizon of darkness.

And what beyond?

His gun was out, held in a hand that shook. He used it to part the curtain, leading slowly with the business end of his weapon.

But what would a gun help? he wondered briefly. How do you kill a man who's already dead?

Still, the gun was what he had, so the gun was what he would use.

He pushed the rest of the way through the dark curtain, the rest of the way into the dead heart of the store.

He took a single step into the dark section at the back. A single step that he didn't even need to take, because he saw what was waiting for him the instant his eyes adjusted to the blackness behind the curtain.

His gun drifted down. There was nothing he could do here. Nothing he could do to stop what had happened, to turn back the clock.

"Tuyen," he said. The word was a sigh, a curse, a prayer all wrapped into one.

The totems were untouched, the articles of blasphemous intent lay all around him just as they always had.

On the back wall, the python gagged on the monkey, which in turn crushed the baby jackal, which then held the tail of the python in its eternal grip. A circle of intimate, painful death that would never end.

Tuyen was in its center. She had been hung with wire to the horrific emblem, thick-gauge silver strands cutting the flesh of her arms and legs. No blood welled from the lacerations, though. And it wasn't hard to divine why. Not hard at all.

Her chest and stomach were bloody. Wounded time after time, stabbed over and over again. Just like –

(*Val*)

– Listings. Just like Geist.

Her throat had been cut.

But that was not all. Apparently Tuyen had earned extra ire from the killer, because in addition to those already-deadly wounds, he had visited one more atrocity on her.

Her eyes had been cut out. Not neatly, not easily. They had been *hacked* out of her skull, so brutally and deeply that Evan could see ragged chips of bone around the edges of the twin pits that had profaned a once-lovely face. The black-and-red gaps stared at nothing and everything and Evan suddenly remembered her in the bar, the first time he had seen her, holding the hand of a drunk and saying, "I've always seen the truth."

Evan's gaze rose from Tuyen's disfigured face. Something was written on the wall above her, above the creature that gorged/gagged/vomited on itself in a despicable circle around her.

Words. They were darker than the dark paint, somewhere between black and brown, and Evan could tell even in the dim light that the killer had used the young woman's own blood to paint the message.

sHe WoNt sEE ANyMor

And just below that, another line. A few more words to seal the message that had already been left in the form of corpse after corpse.

I'LL NEvEr stOP

As he stared at the words, his phone rang. Evan

accepted the call, not bothering to look at the screen to see who it was. He knew.

"I won't, you know," said the familiar voice, the tones flirting with madness.

"Won't what?" said Evan.

"Stop. Much as I want to, I can't." He laughed, and the flirtation became a full-blown love affair. The man's insanity had ceased to be something that defined him. It simply *was* him now. "Not in my nature, I guess. Not after all that's happened."

Evan kept his eyes fixed on the bloody words painted on the wall. "I'm going to figure out a way to end you."

The killer sighed. It reminded Evan of a child's coo, a sound of hope and restrained glee. "That would be nice," he said.

"I'm going to find you."

"That won't be hard. I'll be where this started, where it ends."

"The bar." It wasn't a question. "One hour." He played a hunch, hoping he could gain a measure of power over the unnamed specter that had determined to destroy him. "Who are you?"

"I'm the one you've been looking for."

Evan looked at Tuyen. He didn't want to; could have gone the rest of eternity without ever looking at something like that again. But he felt drawn to her. Her eyes remained sightless gaps, staring at a reality so horrible they had chosen to withdraw. Her body was cut and tortured. Her arms and legs cruelly lashed to the evil totem.

Her hands....

Evan cocked his head. He stepped closer to the back

wall. Closer. Then he was moving so fast it was a marvel he didn't run into anything.

She had something. Her right hand was clenched into a fist. But there was something in it.

"Do you have a name?" he said as he pulled her fingers. Still hoping to get the killer to tell him that bit of information. He believed Tuyen, believed what she had said about the name giving him power. He needed all the power he could get.

"That's not important," said the killer.

Evan felt a pang of irritation that his minor ploy hadn't worked, but only a pang. He was working on getting Tuyen's hand opened. Even in death it was closed so tightly he feared he might have to break her fingers to get at whatever she held. And he knew he would do that if necessary.

"What *is* important," continued the killer, the smile apparent in his voice, "is the look on your wife's face when she died."

Evan stopped moving. The world seemed to hold still for a timeless moment. "Is this a joke to you?" he whispered.

The killer laughed, and this time the smile was gone from his voice. He sounded angry. More than angry, he sounded *wrathful*. "Jokes aren't funny when you know how they end, Evan." He was silent a second, then said, "And I *do* know how this ends," in a voice so low Evan could barely hear it.

Something cracked. Evan realized he had just broken Tuyen's index finger. It jagged out crookedly, as though she was unsure which direction to point. But beneath it he saw a paper. He worked his fingers around it. Pulled.

It came free.

Evan looked at it.

"Are you sure you know how this ends?" he said.

The killer paused. Sounding unsure for the first time, he said, "One hour."

"Why wait?" asked Evan.

A second of silence. Then the killer said, "I agree."

And Evan spun around, because the words hadn't come from his phone.

It came from inside the room.

It came from right behind him.

FIGHT

Evan's face was a mask. Shock, terror, confusion. Feelings familiar and distant, emotions that seemed as though he should know them well, but at the same time could never become comfortable to him.

He realized he must look the way he had looked when he saw Val.

Shock as his world crumbled.

Terror as he wondered how he could have missed what was happening.

Confusion as he asked himself what would happen now.

It all shot through in his mind as he spun, turning from Tuyen's body to the man behind him, the killer who held a knife that still dripped with Tuyen's blood.

The killer slashed out, the knife catching what little light there was in this dark section of the store and glinting like a dark star in a darker night. Evan threw himself to the side, moving quickly enough to avoid being gutted. But only barely.

The guy was fast.

Evan rolled, hearing the air whistle around the return slice as the man reversed his slash and tried again. Another miss, but this one was so close that Evan felt cool air on his cheek as he ducked under the blade.

He had his gun in his hand, and he used it. Pulling the trigger before he had completed his roll.

Boom. Boom-BOOM-*BOOM*.

Each shot was louder in the confines of the back room, each report playing off the one that had gone before, multiplying and becoming more than the sum of its parts. The sound itself was painful.

No way to miss. Not at this range.

The killer shrank back, the hand with the bloody knife up against one ear, bellowing in rage and pain.

Then the scream turned to a laugh as he looked down. The dark coat billowed around him. There was only the darkness of the threads he wore, the black of the air that surrounded them both. There was no blood.

He looked at Evan, a tight grin on his face. For the first time he seemed in control of himself, the madness momentarily fled from his features. That scared Evan more than everything else. Because it meant that whatever was happening, it was something an insane man could understand.

And Evan was trapped here with him. Confined in a world of madness.

The killer's smile gaped, becoming Cheshire-wide, so large it allowed Evan to see every one of the man's teeth. He thought they were stained red as the knife. He wondered if he had feasted on Tuyen's blood. On Listings'.

"You can't kill me," said the man.

He lunged at Evan. Silver flashed before Evan had a chance to react, and Evan screamed as the knife opened a slash on belly.

He clutched himself. Realized that he was still holding something in his hand. Not the gun. Something else.

He looked down.

The killer pulled back his knife. No slashes this time. He was going to stab Evan. Just slam the knife into his stomach or chest, then do it again and again and again until his blood stopped flowing. Just like Geist, and Tuyen, and Listings. And –

(*just like Val*)

– and then he would have won.

He would win.

The knife hovered in space for an instant. A spring, coiled and about to release.

The killer smiled.

The knife thrust forward.

Evan screamed.

KNOWN

"I know your name!"

The knife stopped. It halted as thoroughly and completely as if it had impacted a wall, an invisible force field between Evan and the killer.

The other man stared at him, and for the first time there was neither madness nor that strangely fatalistic calm in his eyes. Now *he* was the one who was confused.

"What?" he said.

Evan held up the paper that he had wrestled from Tuyen's dead hand. It was his business card. Given to her so short a time ago – and yet it seemed so long. More than a lifetime, a million lifetimes. On one side it was just his name and contact information. The boring, basic card the department issued to all detectives.

On the other, a single word. It was smeared, jittery. Traced in the girl's own blood, her own finger for a stylus. She must have written it as she died, written that word and hidden it in death, hidden it in hope.

Just a single word.

A name.

Evan read it again.

Then looked at the killer.

"Hi, Adrian," he said.

The killer's face went through a quick series of expressions: confusion, surprise, hatred.

Fear.

Evan waited for that last one. For the fear. And when he saw it, that was when he shot the sonofabitch.

MEMORIES

The killer – Adrian – looked down again. This time the black of his coat was stained by a darker black of spreading blood. A wellspring of life – or whatever thing he clung to once life had passed – that was pulsing out of him, petering out of him.

Evan watched as the man lurched, one foot going in front of him for balance. He stumbled into a display, knocking over a pile of jars that held God-only-knew-what. Then he sat down hard, his back against a pile of metal shelves. He was breathing fast, his stomach going in and out. Evan could see his breath at his throat as well: a sign of respiratory distress. He'd probably punctured a lung with his shot. A painful, messy way to go as you drowned on your own blood.

He thought of Geist.

Of Tuyen.

Of Listings.

He smiled.

He realized he was still in a half-crouch from when he had rolled away from Adrian's attacks.

Adrian. It was hard to think of him like that. Not as a faceless killer, a monster of the dark. He was someone – or had been, once. Before he became a ghost, a demon come to destroy Evan's life.

Evan felt his legs grow sticky; realized he was still bleeding from the long cut at the base of his stomach. He put a hand against his shirt, shoving the torn fabric against his flesh in a makeshift pressure bandage. The cut hurt, it bled a lot, but it wasn't too deep. And even if it had been a mortal cut, Evan would have stood here and done what he had to do.

Adrian watched him. Wheezing.

Then the wheezing stopped.

Evan looked at the man sharply. Certain the killer must have – what? Died? Gone to the light?

Whatever it he expected, the man wasn't doing it.

He was smiling.

Then... *laughing*.

The laugh was weak, but heartfelt. The giggle of someone who has seen something truly funny. The tinkling chuckle of a man who, alone in the theater, just caught the joke on the screen. The sound infuriated Evan.

"Stop it," he said. "Stop laughing."

Adrian just laughed harder. Blood came up in a frothy wad, choking him. He laughed through it.

"Stop laughing!" But Adrian paid him no heed. Evan wondered if the killer would somehow find a way to win, to destroy him even in death.

Evan's shoulders slumped. He felt the last bit of energy go out of him.

He had nothing left.

The other man *had* won.

"Why?" Evan whispered.

And where screaming had failed, a whisper stopped the other man's bubbling laughter. Tears fell from his eyes, mixing with the blood on his chin. They dripped from his jaw and disappeared into the darkness. He stared at Evan in disbelief, as though incapable of comprehending the question. Then he shrugged. The motion seemed to take most of his energy and he sagged further, dropping a few inches closer to the ground.

"You took what I loved, so I took what you loved," said Adrian. "You killed Val, so I killed everyone else."

Evan's mouth opened.

He fell back. Fell back from Adrian, and then...

... from Val. From her so-sweetly-smiling face as she continues having sex with the man on top of her.

He falls into the hall. Hits his head.

Everything goes black, everything is blank. Like a slate wiped clean, everything once there now gone. The work of his life unraveled and seared away in an instant.

He gets back up. Forces his way into the room. The man has fled. The man –

(*Adrian; I never saw his face, but that's who he is*)

– is gone and Evan is alone with his wife, the once-love of his life. The sliding glass door to the backyard is open and the birds chirp happily because none of them know what's happening here. Or, knowing, don't care.

"You had to find out sooner or later," says Val. Then she pulls the sheets up and hides herself from him. Secrets her body from his eyes. "Close the door on the way out."

Evan leaves. Not for long, and not to close the door.

He comes back a moment later, and now he sees Val's composure, her complete lack of care.

Hard to stay composed when you're staring at a knife.

Even so, Evan doesn't think she really understands

201

what's happening. Or perhaps she understands, but can't really *believe*. Can't believe that something like this would happen to her. To someone else, yes. But not her.

The disbelief protects her. Keeps her brave. Keeps her from screaming.

It stays in her eyes, it shields her. Until the first cut across her throat.

Not too deep. Evan doesn't want her to die. Not yet. He just wants her to feel what it's like to be unable to draw your next breath. To feel what it's like to know everything is about to change.

She claws at the wound. It tears under her fingers, and what was a thin slash becomes a ragged gash. It becomes a second mouth, open wide beneath the mouth that still cannot scream, cannot breathe.

The second mouth seems to be *smiling*.

At the sight of the twice-smile Evan loses it. Completely.

He jumps atop his wife. Just like the man she was screwing. And like that man, he pushes inside her. Only not pleasing flesh, but well-honed steel. Cut after cut, pushing into her chest and stomach, chest and stomach. The knife is –

(*the same one Adrian used on Geist and Tuyen; on Listings*)

– slippery in his hand, but he doesn't stop. Not until Val has disappeared under a sheet of blood. Not until her breasts and stomach are so much meat. Not until she's been stabbed –

(*the same way Adrian stabbed the others*)

– twenty-three times. He counts. He doesn't know why he counts, or why that seems like the right number, but it does. And he doesn't stop until he reaches it. At one point he thinks he hears something, something like a sob from outside. But he doesn't stop. Just keeps pressing the knife down, knife down, knife down. Then looking down...

... at Adrian, who still stared at him, waiting.

"It was you," Evan said. He shook his head. "Did you see?"

The man's face was answer enough. The sheer despair. And Evan knew where the sob had come from. A half-naked man, clenching himself outside a glass door as he heard his lover butchered.

Evan felt himself grow hot again. He had made a mistake. He hadn't meant to kill Val. It was just that smile. That *damned smile*. But that had been his fault. *He* should have suffered. Not everyone else.

He grabbed Adrian and shook the man. "Why didn't you do something? Why didn't you just report it? You could have put me away."

The man laughed. Not the same laugh as before. This wasn't the laugh of a madman leading someone down a river of insanity, the laugh of a man who has won some contest that only he understands. This was a laugh of wretchedness, despair.

Damnation.

"Why didn't I do something?" he said. Then, incredulously, "Why didn't I *do* something?" He spat bloody foam in Evan's face. "I *did*." Then he fell back again. "They swept it under the rug."

Evan let go of Adrian's coat. The man fell back against the shelving with a dull thud, a sound reminiscent of the noise that Listings had made when she flew over the side of the building; bounced off the fire escapes.

It barely registered.

Evan was hearing other things.

Remembering things that had been said, realizing what they really *meant*.

He remembered....

Geist kneeling next to Evan, face to face with someone who meant as much as a son to him. "I've covered for you, taught you, helped you. But I've never lied to you." He paused, and Evan saw a flash of something dark and a little scary in his friend's eyes. "If this is the guy, then we'll catch him. Or kill him."

He remembered....

Listings tossing a devil-may-care smile at him as she knelt and crossed herself. "A girl like me *needs* church: I've probably got more to repent about than most. Some of it has to do with you."

The memories came faster. Faster.

He remembered....

Listings looking into the evidence boxes, the ones that held everything about his wife's murder. So easy to access for the right cop. "I never saw a case move to the cold files so fast," she said. Looking at him, almost as if waiting for him to say something. To confess?

He remembered....

The evidence room. Listings with a look of remorse as she said, "Geist and I tried. We tried our best to keep things moving the way you'd want –"

And he realized she never said she was trying to keep

the case moving forward. She and Geist tried to *stop* it. And they succeeded.

He remembered....

Holding Listings' dying form. Hearing her whisper, "Never told you I knew. Everything." Then her penultimate words: "partners in crime."

Adrian was laughing again. Laughing and crying and coughing all at once, like the universe of his existence had collapsed into the black hole of this moment. "No one listened," he rasped. "But *I* listened. I heard what you did. And I did it to all of them. To everyone who helped you. Everyone you loved."

Evan was pitched back to the bar. To the drunk that Adrian had killed.

What was his name? Ken.

"What about the drunk? Why'd you kill him?"

Adrian's laugh bubbled under a sudden rush of blood. He wiped his lips with a weak hand. Smiling. "I wanted you to listen, Evan. To pay attention to me."

"So you just killed a stranger?"

Adrian looked away dismissively. "He didn't matter. None of them mattered. *No one* mattered after she was gone."

He smiled as though lost in a memory of Val's embrace. The smile made rivers of rage run through Evan's veins. He didn't grow hot, but cold. He wanted to wipe the smile off the smug bastard's face. Forever.

"Adrian?" he said.

The man looked at him. Still smiling. And the smile just grew wider as Evan pointed his gun at his face.

Adrian laughed. The laugh jolted through blood,

through pain. But it was genuinely amused. "You still don't understand, do you? You still don't –"

The sound of the gun silenced the man's laugh, the report cut off his words. The bullet tore through his face and ripped the smile from his flesh.

Evan let out a breath.

"I understand all I want to."

He turned and walked away.

SEEN

Evan walked out of Mystix and down the street, hardly aware of what he was doing and completely *un*aware of what might come next.

What does a man do when his life has ended?

What does a man do when he has seen death come, and killed it?

He found himself in front of a doorway. It was familiar, but he almost didn't recognize it. Everything that had happened to him kept going through his mind over and over, back and forth and back and forth in a never-ending spiral.

Val's death at his hands. Listings' murder.

The fact that Listings and Geist *knew*.

It was all so much. So much that even the neon sign next to the open door barely cued in his mind what he was looking at.

Open door.

Open door.

Neon sign.

He went in. Entered the door that was propped open to catch flies and drunks.

He sat at the bar and was soon nursing a drink. No one questioned him, no one even seemed to notice him. It wasn't that kind of place. And that was good. He needed to be alone, but he couldn't stand solitude right now. He needed to be among other people, even if he had no idea what he might say to them, or what he could ever do to really be a part of them again.

What was going to happen next?

He nursed his drink. He looked at his hands, then looked at his hands again, as though this time he might see something different. As though this time they might hold answers; might tell him where his life had gone and how everything had turned to crap so very quickly.

For the briefest instant it seemed like he was on the edge of an epiphany. An understanding that would shift not merely his perception but his existence.

"I'll read your palm one time," said a voice. *"One time."*

Evan froze. Then turned his head. Slowly.

A man was at the end of the bar. A big guy, dressed in flannels and jeans that had seen lots of wear. Maybe a dock worker. "Can you really do this?" he said, every other word nearly a mumble.

The girl holding his hand nodded. "I've always seen the truth," she said in a tone that was too bright to belong in this bar. Her rainbow hair shimmered like a dream in a dark place.

The drunk laughed. "Tell me a lie. Lies are better."

"No worries," laughed Tuyen. "Whenever people see the truth, they always forget."

Evan's cell rang. The ring tone was one Val had picked. He hadn't changed it yet.

(*Or had he? When did this happen?* What is *happening?*)

"White," he said into the phone.

"Anything?" said Geist's voice. The voice of a dead

man.

Evan sensed motion at the bar's entrance. He spun on his seat. His free hand fell to his belt, brushing past the badge clipped there and circling the grip of the handgun holstered directly behind it.

There was no blood there. No cuts. His shirt was whole.

Why would there be blood? Why cuts?

Rainbow Hair was leaving. *Tuyen* was leaving.

His thoughts swirled. He was in two places at once. Ending and beginning, beginning and end.

"Nothing," he said into the phone. "Haven't seen anything." He didn't know why he was saying it, but felt he must. He had no choice. He sipped at his drink again.

"Well, it was a long shot," said Geist. He sighed. "Don't stay up too late." And then he hung up. He didn't say goodbye.

Evan realized that music was playing on a juke box. "You Spin Me Round" by Dead or Alive. The music ended.

Quarters clinked.

Everything slowed down and became small, like Evan was looking into the wrong end of a pair of binoculars, staring into a portion of space-time that operated at a slower pace.

He could see too much. Too much and at the same time not enough.

He could see.

He could understand.

He heard Tuyen speaking.

"The saddest are the ones who are stuck in a loop...."

And, hearing her, he saw Geist, watching the strange

security footage from Mystix. "Over and over," said the captain with the strange look of someone trying to convey a concept for which there were no words. "The tape loops. It *loops*."

Listings, looking into the evidence boxes: "All these crimes, repeated over and over."

And in the bar, in the here/there and now/then, Evan was still turning, turning. So slow, so far. But faster than he wanted. Closer than he could stand. Understanding at his feet.

Tuyen's voice pushed into his brain, slashed through his thoughts. The voice of a woman who saw. "... never able to influence the world...."

Evan was still turning. Turning.

The women in Mystix. The two old ladies who had ignored him and Tuyen. Because the two old ladies were alive, and never saw the dead walking among them.

Tuyen even said, "They never buy anything from me." And the shadow in the back of the store wasn't another customer, it was the day clerk, the one who ignored him and Listings.

Then they went through the curtain and Tuyen told him, "Some Hmong believe the spirits can't pass through doors. They can appear anywhere, but places with no doors invite them."

Evan realized he couldn't remember actually *going* anywhere since the night at the bar. He could remember *being* places – the street, the church, his house. But he couldn't remember going in or out.

The only places he could remember entering had no

doors.

And the one door he had tried to open – the front door of the church – had remained closed and impassable to him.

Evan's world spun around him, turning in counterpoint as he spun on his barstool.

But what about the killer? The things he did? The things he knew?

And he understood. For a moment he understood. What might happen to a man who wanted vengeance? A man so devastated that he was willing to follow others into a loop. Knowing the truth, knowing the end from the beginning. Knowing his own doom and willing to follow it for the chance to inflict suffering on those who had harmed him. What might such a man be able to do, even as spirit?

There *was* a ghost of vengeance among them. The killer was different. Stuck in the same turning track, following the same paces, but alone of all of them able to touch the real beyond the lie, alone of all of them knowing their world for what it was.

Only the killer had found it more than he wished. The agony of killing, of dying, of living again had driven him mad.

Evan heard Tuyen's voice one more time.

"To be a ghost is to be locked in a lie."

Then he had completed his turn. He had spun around, and was facing back again.

Listings was there.

Evan smiled. He felt something falling away from him. Maybe it was worry, maybe it was fear. For a moment, a single elemental instant, he understood everything. He knew his doom, but knew also that he would at least not be alone.

He was fated always to lose everything... but at least what was lost would then be found once more.

"How many times you gonna listen to that?" he said.

The woman at the jukebox didn't even look at him. "How many times you gonna keep listening to cranks?" she said. Her tones were clipped, almost harsh. Angela Listings, alive once more – or what passed for alive in this existence she shared with Evan and Geist and Tuyen and the killer – punched in the code to start the song again.

"As many times as I have to," said Evan.

The song began, and at the same time it faded. Both there and not, playing in one place, but silent in another. For a few seconds Evan saw reality.

"The saddest are the ones who are stuck in a loop..."

The drunk attacked Listings. Evan watched.

"... replaying the last scenes of their lives over and over..."

Listings never touched her attacker. She couldn't. He was already dead and she didn't know his name.

"... never quite understanding what's going on."

And the killer came. Evan tried to remember his name. He could stop this if he could say the man's name.

But it was gone.

The man wounded both Evan and Listings, and for a single second Evan realized that he had been wounded in the same place at the end. Or was it the beginning?

When did I die? In the bar? In Mystix?

When did the killer die? Here, when I shoot/shot/will shoot him – or in Mystix when I do/did/will do the same thing?

It was all mixed up. All confused.

When your existence is played out on a circle – when you were chasing and being chased by a man on a never-ending track – where is the beginning and where is the end?

Evan shot the killer. Shots that found their marks but did nothing. The killer fled out the open door, into the night.

Evan and Listings ran after him. The blood already gone from their shirts, the wounds knit in their flesh. The end had started, and the beginning was at an end.

They ran through the open door.

And as they followed, Evan thought, strangely, that they were running into a darkness that would never end.

ABOUT THE AUTHOR

Michaelbrent Collings is an award-winning screenwriter and novelist. He has written numerous bestselling horror, thriller, sci-fi, and fantasy novels, including *The Colony Saga, Strangers, Darkbound, Apparition, The Haunted, Hooked: A True Faerie Tale,* and the bestselling YA series *The Billy Saga.* Follow him on Facebook at facebook.com/MichaelbrentCollings or on Twitter @mbcollings.

And if you liked *Crime Seen,* please leave a review on your favorite book review site... and tell your friends!

32710207R00140

Made in the USA
Lexington, KY
30 May 2014